THE WITNESS AT THE GATES

CW01429030

THE WITNESS AT THE GATES

Claudia C. Morrison

iUniverse, Inc.
New York Lincoln Shanghai

THE WITNESS AT THE GATES

Copyright © 2006 by Claudia C. Morrison

All rights reserved. No part of this book may be used or reproduced by any means, graphic, electronic, or mechanical, including photocopying, recording, taping or by any information storage retrieval system without the written permission of the publisher except in the case of brief quotations embodied in critical articles and reviews.

iUniverse books may be ordered through booksellers or by contacting:

iUniverse
2021 Pine Lake Road, Suite 100
Lincoln, NE 68512
www.iuniverse.com
1-800-Authors (1-800-288-4677)

ISBN-13: 978-0-595-40016-4 (pbk)
ISBN-13: 978-0-595-84401-2 (ebk)
ISBN-10: 0-595-40016-7 (pbk)
ISBN-10: 0-595-84401-4 (ebk)

Printed in the United States of America

CHAPTER 1

▼

For Walter it began with a dream about his brother, which he didn't remember until he was in the car fastening his seat belt. Somehow the click of the metal as it snapped into place jarred loose the memory. He sat for a minute, staring at the windshield. When Elizabeth gave him a quizzical look he clenched his jaw and started the engine. Henry, he thought. Damn Henry.

It surprised him to remember the dream: ordinarily he dismissed dreams as garbled nonsense prompted by some bodily malfunction like indigestion, or as the sleeping brain's method of organizing information from the preceding day, **and** tossing out most of it. Either way, dreams were a transient phenomenon that didn't deserve to be taken seriously. People who did take them seriously, or worse, went on about them at length, always irritated him.

In fact, Walter rarely dreamed, springing to consciousness each morning fully alert and ready to meet whatever challenges the day might bring. He had showered and shaved that morning as usual, examining his image in the mirror to see if he needed another haircut. Satisfied that he did not, he had gone downstairs, and while Elizabeth put breakfast together, he stretched out in the patio lounge chair with a cup of coffee and *The Baltimore Sun*, scanning first the headlines, then the markets and the sports section. Stephen had joined him with his orange juice and his latest dinosaur book. Philip was pried away from the television set, and they'd eaten their breakfast. After helping with the dishes, he'd packed the picnic things in the station wagon for their journey to Abbotsford.

Visiting Walter's parents was not the family's favorite weekend excursion, but everyone seemed in a good mood, Stephen and Philip for once not quarreling about who got which side of the back seat. Walter too had been feeling amiable until the snap of the seat-buckle dislodged the dream. Henry would be there at his parents', of course; how could he have forgotten? He grimaced, shifted into reverse, and backed the car out of the drive.

Twice a year, at Christmas and on Independence Day, the Abbott family gathered at the family farmhouse in southern Maryland, across the bay from Annapolis. Jenine took the bus down from Baltimore, Walter drove from Edgewood, and Henry usually returned from wherever he was—when he wasn't in jail, that is. Unfortunately, this summer Henry was out, living less than a mile away, in fact, on the other side of town. He had been living there since Christmas, which was the last time Walter had seen him.

Or rather, the last time he had seen him personally: in reality, Walter saw him five mornings out of every seven, when he drove through the gates of Edgewood Arsenal to get to his office. There Henry would be, standing on the side of the road outside the main gate offering his pamphlets to each car in turn as they queued to go through security. He could repeat Henry's greeting now by heart: "Good morning, I'm from Disarmament Action, how are you today? Might I interest you in some of our literature?" And then, whether he was met with "No Thanks," "Bugger Off," or stony silence, Henry would smile and wish the driver a safe day.

He had been doing this every weekday, rain or shine, for months now, even though his pamphlets were only rarely accepted. Most of the employees looked straight out their windshields and ignored him, their windows closed, their air conditioners running. They hadn't been ordered to do this, there had been no official memo to that effect, but it had been made clear that possession of pacifist tracts wasn't going to get you a promotion. At first a few people had taken Henry's pamphlets out of curiosity, or because his persistence intrigued them. Now it was hard to know what they thought: by common agreement the subject of Henry was avoided. Various government agencies had investigated what, if anything, could be done, but nothing had come of it. The police could make no arrest as long as Henry stayed within the law, which unfortunately he knew well how to do. With no apparent supporters, either in town or within the lab, and with no known connections to any radical organization (his "Disarmament Action" group was apparently a one-man band), Henry posed no threat, unless it was to employee morale. It was uncomfortable having to begin each day rejecting someone, however politely the rebuff was received. It was obscurely humiliating to watch a man persist in making a fool of himself: particularly if that man happened to be one's brother.

Initially Walter had worried that Henry's behavior might affect his job, that it might in particular compromise his security clearance. That hadn't happened, though he had had to put up with some unpleasant teasing from his colleagues at the lab, especially in the early weeks when the subject of "the fruitcake outside the gates" was still a novelty. Walter had grown tired of fending people off with quips about every family having a white sheep. It was a relief when the jokes stopped. Now, by unspoken agreement, no one talked about the man offering pamphlets at the gate.

In the dream he had strangled Henry. He had hit him and knocked him down and then he had leaped onto his back and put his fingers around his neck, squeezing with all his strength. The memory of the feel of his brother's throat under his fingers came back with frightening vividness. He felt a sudden sharp pain in his chest and slowed the car, simultaneously moving his hand to his heart.

"What's wrong?" Elizabeth asked in immediate concern.

"Nothing," he said irritably, "a touch of gas."

"From my pancakes?" she said sarcastically.

"It's nothing, I'm fine," he repeated. The spasm passed. He resumed his normal speed and switched on the radio.

The dial was set to the sports station, where an Orioles/Blue Jays game was underway. Elizabeth gave an audible sigh but the most Walter conceded was to lower the volume slightly. "Please," she objected, "let's have some music, there will be plenty enough games this afternoon." She reached for the dial but Philip, sticking his head between the seats, begged her to leave it where it was.

Elizabeth didn't move her hand. "Put your seat belt on," she said sharply, then added, cajolingly, "Your grandfather will probably be watching the game when we get there, Philip; it will be on most of the afternoon. Until then, why don't we listen to some music that we can all enjoy?"

"That you enjoy, you mean."

"And me too," Stephen put in defensively.

"But Dad and I want to hear the game," Philip persisted. "Don't we, Dad?"

Walter did, but he didn't want to declare himself. It wasn't necessary: Elizabeth gave in, returning her hand to her lap.

Visits to the Abbott farm, for her, were a duty she could happily live without. She never knew how the boys would react to their grandparents, whom they didn't much care for. Philip could sometimes be obstreperous, and/or rude, both of which upset Mrs. Abbott. She reminded herself that Phillip was eleven now and Stephen nine; at least she didn't have to worry about runny bowel movements leaking out of their diaper-stuffed plastic pants onto the brocade spread, or one of them knocking over a lamp, as Philip had done as a toddler, yanking on the cord to find out what would happen. She could still see the look of fascinated astonishment on his face when the lamp crashed and disintegrated, as if it was a revelation to him that things could be turned into a million smaller things that went all over the floor. Later the dog got a sliver of glass in its paw and had to be taken to the vet.

But there was more to her discomfort than anxiety about how the children might behave. Though she had been a member of this family for twelve years, she still didn't feel comfortable with them, any more than Philip and Stephen did. She was never able to relax at Abbottsford, as if she had always to keep up her guard. She didn't feel part of them; she had no role to play but that of an observer. Though even after all these years of observing, she still wasn't sure she understood them: or even liked them, for that matter. Her mother-in-law was usually either morose or irritable, and her father-in-law was a gruff old bear who lived in his den by the flickering light of his television set. Elizabeth did like Jenine, Walter's niece, but affection had so far not been enough to bridge the gulf between them. Jenine was a novice nun, whereas Elizabeth, like her husband, was a resolute atheist. Jenine seemed to her impenetrably, impossibly serene, and serenity was something Elizabeth distrusted.

Then there was Walter's brother, Henry, whom she liked enormously, but it always upset her to think about him. She decided she wouldn't, at least not until she had to.

"Why do they call them the Blue Jays, mom?" Stephen asked, interrupting her thoughts. "Is that Canada's national bird?"

Elizabeth smiled. "Toronto isn't 'Canada,'" she chided, "and as far as I know they don't have a national bird. If they do, it's probably a goose."

"A goose?" Stephen echoed incredulously. "We have an eagle and you have a goose?"

"A wild goose, silly, not one of those dumb things that waddle around in the parks."

"Oh," said Stephen.

Elizabeth looked out the window. Though she didn't much care for the visits, she never tired of the landscape. They were traveling through the countryside of Maryland's eastern shore, which seemed designed on an endearingly human scale. The farms were family-sized, and clearly prosperous, all the barns and silos freshly painted and glittering in the sun. They passed an apple orchard, its attached farmhouse sporting a kidney-shaped swimming pool. The United States was so rich, she thought, and its poor so tidily out of sight, at least in this corner of Maryland. It was a landscape to gladden Jefferson's heart.

"Which side are you on in the ball game, mom?" Stephen prodded, "the Canadians'?"

Elizabeth looked at him in surprise. She couldn't care less about baseball, and she wasn't sure she considered herself Canadian any more, having last lived there thirteen years ago. "I don't see what nationality has to do with it, Stephen," she said, "and you know I don't like taking sides."

"How come you don't like baseball like Dad and Philip?" Stephen pursued, "is it because it's an American game?"

Walter grinned. "Maybe because it isn't a girl's game, dummy," he said over his shoulder.

Stephen gave him a look. "I don't like it much either," he pointed out, "and I'm not a girl."

Elizabeth started to answer, but just then the crowd in the stadium let out a collective moan: the Jays' center fielder had hit a home run.

"Will you people please stop talking," Philip complained. "I can't hear what's going on. Already we're losing."

Elizabeth ignored him. "It's not that I dislike baseball," she said to Stephen, "it's just that I think there are more important things to do in life than play games. Sometimes I think people use games as a way of running away from what's important."

"Like what?" Stephen asked.

"Like this," she said, "talking. Families talking."

"Big deal," Philip said.

*   *   *   *

The Orioles were down three to one when they pulled into the drive. Philip scampered out the minute the car was parked, hardly stopping to let Jenine, who was waiting on the porch, give him a passing hug. "Hey, you, welcome back to Abbottsford," she called as Philip skipped past her. He was on his way to the tv.

"You look wonderful, Jenine," Walter said after embracing her. He meant it sincerely; she was looking radiant. Without her habit and with her hair set free, she was strikingly pretty. Her face always seemed to him shining, but he couldn't tell whether this impression was owing to the brightness of her eyes or because she didn't wear makeup. She reminded him, as always, of Sylvie.

Jenine hugged Elizabeth, then Stephen. "Hi, Aunt Jenine," he said shyly when she released him. "Hi, baby Stephen," she teased, and laughingly took his hand at his ritual protest that he wasn't a baby. It was a standing routine between them; Stephen was small for his age.

Jenine wasn't actually Stephen's aunt but his cousin. She was the daughter of Walter's older sister Sylvie, who was barely twenty when she was killed in an automobile accident, leaving behind her five-month-old daughter. Like Henry and Walter, Sylvie had revolted from the Abbotts' Catholicism in early adolescence; Jenine, however, had adopted it by choice. Why, Walter had never understood: in fact, Jenine's "taking the veil" had so annoyed him he had refused to attend the ceremony. He still rather resented the idea of her being a nun, which seemed to him the waste of an intelligent woman. He kept hoping she would see through the church and leave it, or at least leave her order, but so far she had shown no sign of wanting to. The Sisters of Charity weren't strict—she was allowed to wear street clothes whenever she chose, and she apparently enjoyed the classes she taught at the parochial school in Baltimore that was attached to their "Mother House." Ordinarily Walter despised people who took religion seriously, considering them either weak-minded like his father or filled with delusions like his brother, but Jenine he tended to excuse. She couldn't be accused of either stupidity or dogmatism; she seemed perfectly level-headed, and to her credit, she kept her religion to herself. Altogether she was a bit of a puzzle to Walter; nevertheless, he always enjoyed seeing her.

He went to greet his father, who was in the den watching the ball game. All Walter could see of him was the back of his bald head, whose fringe of gray hairs was getting more ragged by the month. When he received no response to his greeting other than a wave of the hand, he shrugged and headed back toward the kitchen. His mother stood bent over the open oven, basting a roast. "How are you, my son," she said when she looked up and saw him.

He crossed the room and hugged her, then held her away from him to examine her more closely. Her face, flushed from cooking, seemed tired. Her eyes were slightly bloodshot, and wisps of hair were coming loose from her hair net: it was one of her eccentricities to insist on a hairnet in the kitchen. "You look done in, mother," he said, pulling up a chair. "I thought you said you were taking it easy."

Mrs. Abbott had had a hysterectomy in April, from which she had not yet fully recovered. She smiled vaguely, waving her hand in a gesture of dismissal. "I do take it easy. Maybe not all the time, but for the most part," she said.

Elizabeth sat down at the table. Jenine motioned Mrs. Abbott to a chair and patted her on the shoulder. "You should be taking it easy, you know, mom," Elizabeth said. "What's this with a roast anyway? I thought we were having a picnic."

Mrs. Abbott sighed. "I knew we should have called and told you," she said apologetically. "I just thought that with you all going to the fireworks tonight it would be better if we had a sit-down meal. Jenine did most of the cooking. Frankly I'm not up to much these days, everything I do seems to leave me pooped."

Elizabeth glanced at Walter questioningly, at the same time patting her mother-in-law's hand. "There isn't anything new wrong, is there, mother? When did you last see the doctor?"

"Now don't fuss," Mrs. Abbot said irritably, "I was checked out two weeks ago. I'm just under the weather, that's all, I hate it when it's sticky like this."

Walter, willing to be reassured, took her word for it. He leaned back, gazing around the room with satisfaction. Nothing ever changed here; it was the same constant, familiar place, the wood stove in the corner, the varnished pine cabinets, the geraniums on the window sill. "Is Henry here yet?" he asked casually, reaching in his pocket for his cigarettes.

Mrs. Abbott nodded. "Since this morning. He went out for a walk about an hour ago: should be back any time."

Stephen plucked at his mother's sleeve. "Let's go find him, mom," he suggested.

Walter frowned. "Henry will show up when he's ready, he doesn't need finding," he said tartly.

"It's too hot for a walk, Stephen," Elizabeth sighed, "but you go if you like. When will dinner be, Jenine?"

Jenine was washing wine glasses at the sink; she glanced over her shoulder. "Not until four, or a little later, when the game's over. Let's hope it doesn't go into extra innings."

"Baseball," Stephen said, "yuk." Wriggling out from his mother's arm he headed for the door.

The conversation turned to what Walter considered women's pursuits, in this case canning, which Elizabeth claimed she wanted to learn. Walter grimaced when he heard her. Elizabeth was showing alarming signs lately of becoming a vegetarian: every third dinner she served him seemed to be meatless. When he pointed this out, she told him it "felt healthier," a remark which smelled trendy to him. Paranoia about health seemed ubiquitous, wafting in over every air wave, burying him in commercials for bran cereals and cholesterol-free margarine. The country was turning into a nation of hypochondriacs, with idiot bands of joggers and health food fanatics leading the pack. The thought that Elizabeth might be on her way to joining them was unsettling. On the other hand, canning was a topic his mother would take to heart, and teaching her might help her feel needed. Elizabeth was quite skillful at this sort of thing. His grimace turned to grudging admiration. He excused himself and went to the den.

His father was still sitting in his chair, in exactly the same position. Walter wondered for a moment if the old man was asleep with his eyes open. He sat down on the sofa, a long leather affair that made a huffing noise when it took your weight. Philip was sprawled on the floor, less than two feet from the screen. Walter checked the impulse to tell him to move back but changed his mind. It was, after all, a holiday; and he was tired of nagging.

In the game it was the bottom of the fifth, Baltimore at bat. They managed to get two men on with a walk and an infield hit but couldn't produce a run. When the inning was over, Walter turned to his father. "How are things going, Dad," he asked casually.

Mr. Abbott stirred, squelching the leather cushion. "Can't complain," he said gruffly. "We're in the hands of the Lord."

Walter never knew how to respond to such openings, which for him were like closings. When he was thirteen he had tried asserting himself by answering sarcastically, "Which Lord?" His father's response had frightened him. It was before Mr. Abbott became a "born-again," back when he was still a Catholic, but his reaction had been ferocious. Normally his father was very controlled, but from then on Walter had thought of him as a reservoir of some secret, powerful, violence. The fact that it was concealed made it even more alarming, for you never knew exactly how much of it there was. An explosion, if it came, might be as awful as murder.

"Does that mean your life can't be improved, or that you're reconciled to things as they are?" he asked. He chose his words and tone carefully, not wanting to pick a fight, but feeling compelled, as always, to deconstruct his father's clichés.

Mr. Abbott was more secure in generalities. "I mean we're in the hands of the Lord and that I've nothing to complain about," he repeated, as if it had been clear enough the first time.

"Ah, well, good," Walter said, giving it up.

They turned back to the game, which Mr. Abbott appeared to be enjoying, in his own stolid way. Walter smiled, remembering how years ago Stephen, at age five, had said he should be called grumpa, not grampa. When the shortstop made a heroic effort or the catcher threw a man out, he called out hoarse praise. Philip also cheered winning moves, but grew furious at the umpire for unfavorable calls and berated the pitcher, Boddicker, when he gave up a hit. When he walked two men in a row to lead off the sixth, Phillip stood up, shook his fist at the screen, and called him a dumb sonuvabitch. Walter opened his mouth to reprove him, but before the words formed, Philip's anger had changed to a cheer: Boddicker had induced Martinez to hit into a double-play. The next batter was an easy strikeout.

"You shouldn't get so angry, Philip," Walter admonished mildly during the commercial. "Games aren't over till the last inning."

Mr. Abbott twisted in his seat. "Leave the kid alone," he said, "part of the fun of the game is letting off steam."

Walter, startled, was immediately annoyed. It went without saying that adults should maintain a common disciplinary front before children, a rule his father had just violated. He wondered briefly if he was trying to score points with Philip, competing with his own son for his grandson's favor. If so, it was pathetic.

"Though most likely I said the same thing to you when you were his age," Mr. Abbott added. It was a concession of sorts. The tone wasn't exactly gracious, but Walter allowed himself to be mollified.

∗   ∗   ∗   ∗

Once outside, Stephen was happy. He loved Abbottsford, especially in the summer. His parents called it a farm but it wasn't really, not one with animals and crops. His mother had explained that his grandfather bought it because he liked the view. The land around was mostly meadow and fields, with clumps of trees scattered about and an apple orchard behind the house. A stream ran through it into the woods, which is where Stephen guessed he would find his uncle; Henry had shown him a special place there two summers ago.

The previous summer Henry hadn't come to Abbottsford; why, Stephen didn't know. He remembered asking both his mother and his grandmother, but neither would say more than "He couldn't come this year," in a tone that discouraged further questions.

He stopped in the orchard and examined a few windfall apples. The wormy ones, or ones with pulpy spots, he discarded. There was one almost-perfect one, which he shined on his shirt and put in the pocket of his shorts.

The stream ran beside a path for a good distance, but not all the way; if you wanted to follow it to the end you had to wade it, barefoot. At the end of the path, he took off his sneakers and hung them around his neck. The water was ankle deep, and so clear where the sun shone you could see the pebbles and stones of the bed beneath. He temporarily lost interest in finding Henry and crouched down to look at them.

He had always been fascinated with stones, which after dinosaurs were his favorite things. His mother also liked them; it was one of the hobbies they shared. She had asked the man who designed their house to build in glass display cases in the entrance hall where she kept their collections, hers and his. Her stones, of course, were much fancier, particularly the ones she'd bought from collectors. The only one in the glass cases she found herself was a smooth egg-shaped agate displayed on blue velvet. Last Christmas she had given Stephen a small stone-polishing machine, but he hadn't done much with it. It took forever to make the stones really smooth; he decided he preferred them the way they were.

He selected a handful that looked interesting and sat down on the bank, leaving one foot in the water so he could feel it running over his toes. He spread the stones out to examine them, but it was hard to judge whether they were special enough to keep. Stones were always prettier when they were wet; it made the colors deeper. After they dried, some of them looked boring, which always surprised him.

So far, the day had gone fairly well, though it was too bad the picnic wasn't until tomorrow; you could eat an indoors roast any time. But they'd be going to the fireworks later, and Aunt Jenine had shown him the peach pie his grandmother had baked that morning especially for him. Philip's favorite was apple, which was what they had last year; Stephen's was peach. He wondered why people had different favorites, and why he and Philip never seemed to like the same things. Sometimes he played a fantasy game in which Philip turned out to be somebody else's brother, that he'd been mixed up in the hospital and his true brother was walking around in another family somewhere. True brothers, Stephen felt, would share things.

He took out his apple and rubbed it on his sleeve. He opened his mouth to bite it when he felt someone watching him from the other bank. "I trust you're saving some of that for me," a voice said with mock sternness.

A skinny, bearded man wearing jeans and a plaid work shirt emerged from behind a tree and waded across the stream. Stephen recognized him more from his voice than from his appearance: the last time he had seen Henry, he didn't have a beard. "Hi, Uncle Henry, were you spying?" he asked.

Henry splashed across the stream. "Right," he said, "I'm with the CIA." He pointed his fingers at Stephen and made the noise of a machine gun. "I'm Rambo, come to purge the world of evil: Rat-a-tat-tat."

"You're crazy, Uncle Henry," Stephen giggled.

"Am I," Henry said, his eyes wrinkling with a smile. He stretched out on the bank beside Stephen, his hands behind his head.

Stephen wasn't used to seeing people making themselves comfortable without first saying how are you and all the rest. He liked this about Henry, but it took getting used to. "What have you been doing out here?" he asked.

Henry considered. "Nothing much," he said, looking up at the sky. "Breathing in the air, enjoying the view. The clouds are pretty dramatic today, have you noticed?"

Stephen cast a critical eye upward. Through the space between the trees the sky was a brilliant blue, with puffy masses of white drifting through it. He shrugged. "Is that really all you've been doing, looking at clouds? I've been looking for stones."

Henry nodded. "I checked for those too. Here, these are for you." He reached into his pocket and pulled out three good-sized pebbles, one gray with jagged green lines, one almost pure pink, and the third a pretty quartz with mustard-yellow glints. Stephen took them in his hand and looked them over carefully, lining them up with his own.

"So what have you been doing this year, Uncle Henry," he asked, to be polite. "Where are you working?"

"No one place," Henry answered comfortably. "I do odd jobs here and there, carpentry, painting—you know, Handy-Andy work. I fix things. You need anything fixed?"

Stephen shook his head. "Are you still living out west?"

"In Kentucky? No, I don't live there any more."

Stephen waited. "Well, where then?" he asked.

Henry rolled over on his elbow and looked away, as if deliberating. "I'm living in Edgewood now, Steve," he said finally, "I've been there for the better part of a year."

At first Stephen thought he hadn't heard right. "Then why haven't you been to see us?" he demanded. "Nobody told me you were there. Why don't I ever get told anything?"

Henry met his glare. "I suppose because they think you're too young to understand certain things," he said levelly.

"Like what?"

"Complicated things, like politics and ethics, and how confusing they can be. Like the kinds of psychological conflicts people get into with each other, which they usually don't understand themselves."

Stephen frowned. "I think that's bull shit," he said after a while. "It's just another excuse for nobody ever telling me anything. Just because I'm a kid doesn't mean I'm stupid. You're as bad as my mom and dad."

Henry thought about this. It was another reason Stephen liked him, that he accepted what you said without getting upset about it, or carrying on about the language you said it in.

"If I'm hiding behind any excuse, it's that I'm not your father, Stephen. The reason you haven't seen me is that I haven't been invited to your house, and if you want to know why not, I think you should ask your father. I don't think he'd like me explaining his decisions to you."

"Why not?" Stephen protested. "Aren't you his brother?"

Henry smiled. "Even with brothers you need permission. Look, let me say this: I'm living my life in what I think is the right way, but your father doesn't see it like that. We disagree, and because of that he doesn't like seeing me much, except here at Abbottsford where we call a truce for your grandmother's sake. Now, why don't we talk about something else? I've about had my say on this subject. Tell me what you've been doing this year: what are they teaching you at your school, anything useful?"

Stephen sniffed. He didn't want to talk about school, he wanted to know what Henry and his father disagreed about. He hated it when adults treated him with condescension, smoothing things over with words that left things just as mysterious as before. He didn't answer.

Henry studied him. When his silence persisted, he suggested they start back to the house. Stephen didn't want to do this either. At the house he would have to share Henry with the others. He wanted Henry to stay, but at the same time he wanted him to go. What he really wanted was for him to prefer staying, but he couldn't say that. "I'm going to look for more stones," he said instead, "dinner won't be for hours."

Henry regarded him evenly. "Well, it's time for me to get back, whatever it is for you. You come or stay as you like."

He stood up and waded out into the stream. Stephen remained stubbornly on the bank.

CHAPTER 2

▼

Elizabeth lay on the porch swing fanning herself with the latest issue of *Newsweek*. Behind her she could hear the reassuring sounds of the ball game, reassuring because as long as it was on, she could more or less count on being alone. She had just finished reading an article about a new form of cocaine on the market, something called crack. She had the feeling she had read another article like it in a different magazine a few weeks ago. It was curious, she thought, how the media were always pushing the same causes at the same time. Last year it was terrorism and Col. Khadafi; this year it was drugs. Some hotshot basketball star at the University of Maryland had recently died of an overdose, the latest in a series of high-profile deaths. With mid-term elections not far off, drug abuse was a sure-fire issue, particularly the way it was presented on television. The pictures she had seen of cocaine-addicted babies, scrawny, wizened little things twitching all over and going into convulsions, were horrifying.

The babies bothered her, but so did the way the politicians were manipulating the issue. Nancy Reagan had been drumming it for months, and Ronny could be counted on to mount the bandwagon any time. When he did, she thought, watch out: there would be another spasm of militant American righteousness, another witch-hunt at the OK Corral.

She stifled a yawn. It crossed her mind to get up and make herself a glass of iced tea, but she was too enervated to move. Even in the shade of the porch the heat was overpowering. Sunlight seemed to invade from all directions, bouncing up from the floorboards and down from the ceiling. She resumed fanning herself. Walter would no doubt disagree with her about this Newsweek article, and dismiss her views as one of their American/Canadian differences. It was an attitude she resented. She had minored in American history at the University of Toronto and though she was certainly no authority, she prided herself on her knowledge of it. U.S. history had always intrigued her; it was so much bloodier and more dramatic than Canada's, which was by comparison all fur trade and railroads. One thing she found extraordinary was how every decade or so the people of the United States seemed to get swept up in some kind of holy crusade, starting at the very beginning of their history with the Puritans attacking the colony at Merrymount and chopping down the Maypoles. The enemy's name changed over the centuries——witches, Indians, abolitionists, anarchists——but the hue and cry remained the same: purge the country of its Communists, junkies, or whatever, and the Lord's kingdom would be realized. Now they were declaring a holy war on drugs, which seemed to her astonishingly stupid.

It amazed her that Americans, of all people, should pretend to be ignorant of the law of supply and demand. They were making no attempt to dry up the demand for drugs, probably because they saw it as futile, but as long as the demand was there, any attempt to keep drugs off the market was useless, for as soon as one dealer was arrested, another simply took his place. It seemed obvious that as long as there was money to be made——and for thousands of people the only money that could be made——there would never be a shortage of dealers. Besides, she thought, flipping the magazine back on the table, what on earth did the politicians think would happen if they succeeded in drying up drugs? It would be a recipe for chaos: what else was keeping the lid on ghetto rage? And if the price of getting stoned suddenly skyrocketed, so would crime.

On the other hand, she had to admit that this new form of cocaine the article was talking about did seem rather awful, not at all like marijuana, her own generation's instrument of consciousness-change. Apparently this "crack" was as addictive as heroin. In any case, it wasn't something she wanted Philip or Stephen trying.

She sat up, startled by the thought that cocaine dealers might already be showing up at Philip's junior high. But surely that was paranoid? It was frustrating that she couldn't be sure; it seemed harder all the time to sort out what was media-hyped and manufactured from what was real. If it was actually true that pushers might be coming to small-town Maryland schools, she and Walter should be doing something, warning the children, at the very least.

The prospect depressed her. The subject of drugs was something they had argued about for years, arguments resolved by her outwardly conceding the point while privately doing as she pleased. In practice, this meant smoking a joint every now and then at her sister's in Baltimore, with friends from pre-Walter days.

Walter passionately opposed marijuana, and had in effect forbidden her smoking it, on the grounds that if she was ever caught "using drugs," as he put it, he would lose his security clearance, and with it his job. "Just what I need," he had said once, sourly, "a fruitcake for a brother and a pothead for a wife."

Elizabeth disliked his calling marijuana a "drug," which to her way of thinking meant something addictive. Marijuana wasn't addictive; study after study had confirmed that. It was a mild mood-elevator, and preferable to alcohol for any number of reasons. Having a joint now and then caused no social harm that she could see, nor could she fathom how her occasional indulgence harmed Walter, especially if she only indulged when she was out of town, where he didn't know about it. So she continued to do as she pleased.

The drug problem wasn't the only thing bothering her; there was also the matter of what Walter did for a living. She had never wanted him to take this job; in fact, way back when he'd just finished his degree, she'd pleaded with him not to, but he refused to listen, pointing out that it was the highest-paying offer they had received, and that with all his university debts, this was no minor consideration. Moreover, he liked the location: he wouldn't be far from his parents' farm, and they would be less than two hours from either Washington or Baltimore if they developed a sudden craving for a big city. The job itself he defended by arguing that research into chemical weapons was purely for deterrent purposes, so that anyone thinking of using such weapons against America would know they would be repaid in kind. He had also argued that the current stock of chemical weapons existed in an unstable and dangerous form, and that it would be a service to humanity if a weapon could be perfected that posed no danger in peacetime. The new binary model he would be working on would be just that, he said, it would be invulnerable to accident unless and until the component gasses were deliberately mixed, which they wouldn't be unless a war had started and the weapon was sanctioned by the proper chain of command. He argued, finally, that not taking the job "on moral grounds" (which were relative, in any case) was a futile gesture, since someone else was bound to take his place.

She had allowed such arguments to persuade her. They had been married less than a year then; Philip was just six months old, and she was in love with motherhood. She wanted the marriage to work, and the promise of lifetime security with a more than comfortable salary exerted no small appeal. There had been another attraction, though she hadn't liked to admit it, namely, that she had in a way liked the idea that Walter would not be able to talk about his work, which was Top Secret; as if she had known intuitively that the less she knew about it the better.

It was easier then to put aside her scruples; the weapon Walter was working on at the time had been purely experimental, which to Elizabeth was next door to imaginary. It had never seemed quite real, not even after the breakthrough three years ago that apparently made the design technically feasible. When Congress passed the bill authorizing Bigeye's deployment, which they did only last winter, her original moral queasiness resurfaced. The bombs were in production now; they were no longer an abstraction.

She wondered how much Henry was to blame for her renewed concern about Walter's work. She hadn't talked to him in over a year (Walter had made it plain that he wanted her to have nothing to do with his embarrassing brother), but she had read one of his pamphlets, which she had found one week when she borrowed Walter's car while hers was at the shop. It was crumpled up on the floor of the back seat, where she assumed Walter had tossed it. She had straightened it out and read it, and then reread it; it suddenly made her aware how much she had been avoiding the issue, how she in effect had for years been doing a Scarlet O'Hara number, saying "I'll think of all that later, at Tara," meaning some time in the ever-receding future.

She glanced across the lawn to the gentle green hills beyond the field. So here she was, she thought sardonically, seated on a porch at an imitation Tara: it was high time to do some of that thinking.

But Walter suddenly appeared in the doorway. "What are you doing out here?" he asked, "where's Mom and Jenine?"

He sat down beside her, a cigarette in his hand. She took a drag from it and handed it back. She had given up smoking six months ago, but she still couldn't resist a puff now and again; Walter's refusal to quit meant they were always available. "Your mother's gone up for a nap and Jenine is out meditating or something in the garden," she said.

"So, what have you been doing?"

Elizabeth leaned back in the swing. "Nothing much. Imagining I was on the verandah at Tara. Southern porches remind me of *Gone With The Wind.*"

"Great," Walter said amiably, "I've always wanted to be Rhett Butler——or am I Ashley Wilkes in this production?"

A picture of her brother-in-law crossed Elizabeth's mind. She changed the subject. "I've been reading that *Newsweek,*" she said, poking it with her foot. "There are all sorts of alarms out about this new drug called crack. We should have a family council and talk about it with the boys. What do you think? Unless it's all yellow journalism, crack dealers could be showing up any day now."

Walter glanced at the cover. "You're right," he said, "we'll do it when we get back. But I thought they taught them about this stuff in school. Don't they?"

Elizabeth didn't know; she assumed they did, but she wasn't sure. She made a note to ask Stephen. Suddenly there was a whoop from the living room. "Dad, come quick, Ripken's hit another homer," Phillip cried. Walter rolled his eyes but went back inside.

Elizabeth, alone again on the swing, wondered what was keeping Henry. She wanted to talk to him, preferably away from the rest of the family. Walter wouldn't like it, it would probably raise the tension in this odd family yet another notch if it was discovered, but at the moment she didn't care: she had to get off this swing. She slipped out the screen door, closing it noiselessly behind her.

✳   ✳   ✳   ✳

Between the orchard and the woods there was a small secluded patch of field Henry would cross on his way to the house. She sat down at its edge in the shade of an oak tree, resting her back against the trunk. The field, a thick tangle of mid-summer clover spotted with daisies, shimmered in the glare, as if the heat was coming not from the sun but from the earth and the plants themselves. It was astonishingly hot, even in the shade. All these years of living in Maryland, and she still wasn't used to it.

She closed her eyes and tried to concentrate on the sensation. For the past few months she had been taking a workshop in Zen meditation at the local community center. "Pay attention to whatever it is you are experiencing," their *dashi* had counseled. "If what you feel is boredom, feel it fully; if anxiety, look it straight in the face. The point is to observe, without judgment." She wondered if this would work with the heat.

She crossed her legs in a half-lotus position and tried to make her mind go blank, refusing to hold on to words, particularly judgment-freighted ones, focusing instead on the sense of being enveloped in warmth. Enveloped was better than blanketed, to say nothing of suffocated, but with or without words, the sensation was unpleasant. It wasn't like a sauna or sunbathing on a beach: this heat seemed to suck moisture from every pore, coating the skin with a film of perspiration, draining every ounce of energy. She could feel her shoulders slumping, as if she was sliding into a steam bath, or a swamp. She caught herself and opened her eyes. She was half-expecting to see Henry, but there was nothing in front of her but the field of clover, shimmering in the heat haze.

She resumed her meditative posture, wishing she had the meditation pillow she had recently purchased. Elizabeth was new to the practice of meditation; the workshop had been suggested to her by a woman named Arlene whom she had met at the PTA, who had assured her that Zen was a technique, not a religion. There were gurus, she said, but they never made any moves to convert you. The point was to attain *satori*, or enlightenment, but even if you never made it that far, the practice was still good for your health. It calmed the mind, Arlene said, it gave you inner poise.

Elizabeth closed her eyes. At first she saw only blackness haloed by a circle of light, which she recognized as the obverse image of the sun. She stared into its center, trying to concentrate on the circle of darkness, but the fringe around it glowed yellow and orange and began pulsing in small waves, and in its pulse she felt a strange, erotically tinged yearning. At the same time the darkness shaded into an image of Henry, smiling his slow, slightly crooked smile. She seemed to see him standing on the bank above her, looking down.

The sudden shrill whine of a mosquito punctured the dream. She watched it land on her forearm, quickly crushing it before it could draw blood. Even so, it left a small red trail. She licked it clean and glanced across the field.

The images she had seen puzzled her. Why had she imagined Henry smiling at her approvingly, and the pulsing aura of desire? It was absurd, she had never thought of Henry in sexual terms. He wasn't bad-looking, but he was embarrassingly awkward—loose-jointed and shambly, his shoulders hunched inward, protecting his chest. He had had asthma since childhood and breathed through his mouth. This, more than anything, made him sexually off-putting; people who went around with their mouths half-open couldn't help but look stupid. Henry wasn't, of course, but there was something eccentric in his manner, as if he never learned how to compose his face into the proper social mask. He smiled readily enough, though not necessarily when you expected him to, but when he wasn't smiling, his face lapsed into a blank neutrality that was difficult to read. It made people wary of him, as if his refusal to adopt the proper facial expression signaled that he couldn't be depended on to follow the rules in other areas either. This was true also of the way he spoke. When you asked him a question, no matter how ordinary or conventional, he seemed to ponder it for an inordinately long time before answering. When finally he did reply, his language was straightforward, but for all its directness it sounded curiously artificial, as if each phrase had been too carefully weighed beforehand.

Elizabeth sighed. He was altogether a queer duck, her brother-in-law. At the same time, he was the only member of the family she consistently found interesting. Did she desire him now too, was that to be part of the mix? She grimaced. Such a fantasy was a product of the heat, surely, together with the stifling atmosphere of Abbottsford. Walter's family sometimes made her want to blow things sky high, out of sheer perversity. Whatever else an affair with Henry might accomplish, it would certainly accomplish that.

She reminded herself that she had no intention of doing such a thing, that she merely wanted to talk to him. There were questions she wanted him to answer, like what he hoped to gain by standing outside the Arsenal gates every morning, why he was being so stubborn when he must know his protest was futile. She wanted him to tell her what he hoped to accomplish, and if he agreed that he was accomplishing nothing, she wanted to persuade him to stop. There was also the question of his motive, which mystified her. Had he reverted to his childhood Catholicism, was that why he stood out there every day handing out leaflets nobody wanted? Was he doing it for God's sake, or as a way to work out some private guilt? Perhaps Walter was right in saying that his brother was a hopeless masochist, though he might equally well be some kind of apprentice saint, for all Elizabeth knew. He could also be acting out of a private spite against his brother: how did one distinguish these things?

Her mind felt rubbery. Again her eyelids drooped, and she slid into a doze. As if in an out-of-focus film, she saw herself wading in a stream. Here and there her eye kept catching glints and sparkles of gold, but she couldn't see how deep it was, her view was obscured by masses of ferns which leaned over the water as if trying to drink with their fronds. She pushed them aside, and saw a small gold nugget half-buried in the sand. She picked it up, then, feeling in the mud, unearthed another, and another. She rinsed them carefully and held them up to the sun before putting them in the breast pocket of her blouse, which is where her hand still was when she looked up and saw Henry standing on the bank. "You don't intend to keep all those, do you?" he asked.

The question so startled her she opened her eyes. It took her a moment to separate reality from the dream, but when it did she saw that the figure coming across the field was not a mirage, but Henry. He had seen her. He was waving.

When he came up to her she didn't know at first whether or not to hug him, fearing it might prove awkward, but then she did and it felt right, neither too prolonged, which would have been confusing, nor so brief as to be purely formal. She wondered what her body felt like to him. His had seemed shockingly thin; for the brief seconds she held him she was conscious mainly of the sharpness of his bones.

"You've lost weight, Henry, are you well?" she asked when they drew apart, but looking at him she saw that touch had been deceptive. He was deeply tanned, and looked healthier than she had seen him in a long time.

"Quite well, thanks. You?"

"Fine," she answered, but the word seemed inadequate. "Embarrassed," she added. "It's been so long, Henry, we should have called, written…"

Anyone else would have accepted the apology and smoothed things along, but Henry regarded her levelly and didn't answer. The effect was to make her feel more deeply the truth of what she had said. Of course they should have called, she thought with a pang, it was not conscionable for brothers to live in the same town and make no attempt to communicate. "It's Walter, you know," she said hastily, "you upset him, Henry, and he doesn't like being upset. He said he didn't see the point in seeing you, that it caused too much conflict."

"Well, he's probably right there," Henry replied amicably. "Don't let it worry you, Elizabeth, you needn't explain." He sat down beside the tree, motioning her to resume her seat. "What brings you out here?" he asked. "Were you enjoying the heat wave, or did someone dragoon you into fetching me?"

She smiled. "Not fetch exactly: waylay would be more like it. It was my idea. I wanted to talk to you."

He gave her a quizzical look. "I read one of your pamphlets, Henry," she explained, "and of course I know about your vigils. I mainly wanted to ask why you do it——why you keep doing it, I mean. As well as finding out how you are and how life is for you, and all the rest of it."

She stopped, conscious of the pressure of time. Henry, however, responded as if time was no consequence. He stretched out on the grass with his hands behind his head and considered what she had said. "First of all," he answered, "my health is good, I'm quite happy, I have no particular complaints. As to my vigils at the Arsenal, I feel very strongly that creating chemical weapons is morally wrong, whether the weapons are intended for defense or offense. The argument put forward that because the Russians possess them, we should too, makes no sense to me. They are indiscriminate killers, and in preparing to use them we put ourselves morally on a par with the Communists, to say nothing of risking the lives of millions of people." He paused. "But if you've read the pamphlet, you know all this."

Elizabeth nodded.

"I gather then that your objection is pragmatic. My daily vigils no longer 'serve a purpose' and should therefore stop. This implies that leafletting at a chemical warfare research center once is all right——to draw attention to the cause, say, but that to keep it up accomplishes nothing, or worse, alienates people. Am I right?"

Again Elizabeth nodded.

"It's getting close to dinner," he said, "but, briefly, let me try to explain my position. First, I don't think we should make quick judgments about the short-term effectiveness of any particular non-violent protest since its intention is to bring about a change in peoples' hearts, which is a long-term process. Whether an action 'works' or not is ultimately not in one's hands: if change occurs as a result of what I or others do, well and good, but that isn't the whole its purpose. Pacifist action also involves what the Quakers call 'witnessing to the truth'."

"The truth?" Elizabeth interrupted archly, "is that with a small t or a capital one?"

"I think the Quakers meant it with m o r a l in front of it. They were the first people in this country to protest against slavery, did you know that? There was one wonderful old Quaker around the time of the Revolution who chained himself to a tree for a month every year, outside the meeting house in Philadelphia. When members of the congregation passed and saw him, they'd come over and offer to release him, or bring him food and water. He'd thank them for their concern, and then add that he was surprised they weren't abolitionists if his condition bothered them so much, since chattel slavery involved heavier chains than his. How many converts he made isn't recorded, and I'm not sure it matters. To a pacifist what matters is not a "victory" where good scores immediate gains, but that there should be some good present somewhere—'if only to leaven the loaf,' as Thoreau later put it."

Elizabeth, listening, found his mild, serious tone disconcerting. Among the people she knew, moral concern was considered naive, something slightly quaint, if not downright childish. Henry's tone was disarming, but she resisted his idealism. Ideals were abstractions, and she was wary of abstractions. "That sounds very nice, Henry, but matter to whom? To God, to some abstract concept of humanity? To whom?"

He glanced at her with surprise, and a glint of admiration. "Not to God," he said, "I've no idea what people mean by God. Perhaps it matters to man's image of himself—to my image of him, at any rate. But I think you misunderstood me, Elizabeth, I'm not ruling out change as a goal of non-violent action, only saying that that's not the sum of its purpose. Whether the researchers at Edgewood Arsenal have a change of heart as a result of what I'm doing and quit their jobs is a matter between them and their consciences. I do believe that if Americans knew what these weapons are capable of they would want their government to stop making them. Unfortunately, the public is not very well informed. Pacifists don't presume to tell people what to do, you know, only urge them to educate themselves and express themselves politically."

He paused. "You are asking me to concern myself with ends," he said, "rather than means. There's an old sixties slogan which maybe you remember: 'There is no way to peace, peace is the way'? That's all I'm doing at Edgewood—witnessing for peace, witnessing against violence. I'm not going to keep it up forever, though: I promised myself that I'd try this for two years, and that if there were no signs of change at the end of that time, I'd do something else, like camp outside the White House or something."

She was struck by his apparent indifference to what she or anyone else might think of his vigils. Two years of being an outcast was a long time. "Surely you care whether people respond to you positively or negatively, Henry," she objected.

He grinned. "I think you mean, 'Why do you allow yourself to be humiliated day after day, Henry,' right?"

"Yes, perhaps I do," she said levelly. "Why do you? Doesn't it bother you?"

He shrugged. "In one way, yes, in another, no. People's responses to non-violent witness are as individual as they are. Feeling anger towards me because I'm asking them to think about things they don't want to think about is a natural response, initially at least. Who knows? Maybe they first have to go through a stage of despising me, which then makes them reflect on why they feel that way: maybe that's part of how change comes about. I sometimes think when I'm standing out at the gates that I'm kind of like a public Rorschach test, or like the psychiatrist who sits behind his desk not saying anything, just letting the patient hear his own words and reflect on them. Maybe what I'm doing is some kind of guerrilla psychotherapy."

He was teasing, but Elizabeth found his answer irritating. "That's a bit presumptuous, don't you think, Henry?" she asked coolly.

"Sorry," he said, momentarily confused by her change of tone. His changed accordingly. "Let me try again," he said softly. "I leaflet at Edgewood Arsenal as a witness to the truth as I see it, and the truth as I see it is that the production and stockpiling of nerve gas should be outlawed. If this belief makes people angry, I hope it's because I have troubled their consciences, because in my view their conscience should be troubled. What my government is doing with my tax dollars is wrong, and if I believe that—since I believe that—I have an obligation to do what I can to communicate it."

"Even if people are troubled to no purpose?" Elizabeth said quickly. "I'm sorry, Henry, I can't see the morality in stirring up bad feeling when it does nothing to solve the problem. How can you be so sure you are right? Where does your certainty come from?"

"Not from the church, if that's what you mean," he replied. "The source of my 'certainty,' I guess, is simply my awareness of right and wrong, which may have had its origins in being raised a Catholic, but that's not only it. Let's say it's a product of my attempt to take life seriously. If my conclusions are wrong, I trust my commitment to non-violence will keep my error within bounds. But don't you find it curious, Elizabeth, that my protest against these weapons apparently stirs more concern in you than the weapons themselves? Why is that, do you think?"

The question disconcerted her. Why, after all, was she arguing? She agreed with him that working on these new chemical horrors was wrong. God knows the U.S. military had seventy-nine varieties of ways to kill people as it was, they didn't need to add fancy new poisons to the stockpile. Henry was right; but the consequences of agreeing with him frightened her. She felt a vague dread, followed by the odd thought that maybe she was living with the wrong brother, living, so to speak, on the wrong side of the gates....

"Henry," she said distractedly, "what do you think I should do?"

Her unexpected earnestness touched him. She was sitting with her back to the sun, the light glinting on her hair, which half-fell over her face as she lowered her head. She seemed very vulnerable, like a small animal with a wounded limb. "I'm not sure exactly what you are asking, Elizabeth," he said slowly, "but maybe you should start with trying to take the world more seriously, trying to take your life more seriously...." He stopped, feeling both inadequate and hypocritical. Behind her question lay deeper issues that he was not acknowledging. "Come," he said gently, "it's not as bad as that. I know your position isn't easy, and I can't presume to advise you. Just do what you think is right, Elizabeth. Follow your heart."

She looked at him sharply. "Damn it, Henry, I wouldn't say things like that if I were you," she retorted. "What would you do if I told you that if I followed my heart right now I'd be trying to seduce you?"

It made him react, as she had intended it to. Under the circumstances her words were shockingly bold, and would no doubt later make her ashamed. She didn't care. For a instant she thought she glimpsed a flash of arousal in his eyes, but he lowered them too quickly for her to be sure. "Sorry, I should have said follow your conscience," he said wryly, and standing, held out his hand. "Come, mom's waiting, and so is Walter."

She allowed him to pull her to her feet, on the whole relieved that he had chosen to make light of her question. "You're a cool one, brother-in-law," she said as they walked back to the house. "If you weren't so bloody moral, I'd say you should go into politics."

Henry chuckled. "Not my style: that's more like Walter's trip."

"Do you dislike him, Henry?" she asked suddenly.

"No," he answered simply. "He's my brother."

"But you obviously don't approve of him."

"No."

What happened next was something neither of them would have predicted; afterwards, they could hardly believe they had behaved as they did. Just before they reached the house, Elizabeth impulsively put her hand on Henry's arm and restrained him. She wanted to apologize, she said, that they had so few occasions to talk to each other, as human beings rather than as "in-laws." "I wish I knew you better, Henry," she said, in a tone more plaintive than she intended.

To her surprise—and, she suspected, to Henry's—he responded with an impulse of his own. He took from his pocket a small notebook, a "sort of diary," he said, which he had been writing in it when Stephen came upon him. If she really wanted to know him better, perhaps it would help. She thanked him and accepted it, feeling honored that he would confide in her this way: a diary was so personal a thing. "It's no big deal," he said with a shrug, "it's mostly political reflections. You may well find it boring."

She smiled and slipped it in the pocket of her skirt, but as they mounted the porch steps, the feel of it against her thigh made her uneasy. She had taken a step she would not normally take, and she didn't know where it would lead.

CHAPTER 3

▼

"Don't scold him, Daddy," Jenine said in a cajoling voice, "it's my fault for having made that popcorn."

Elizabeth, sitting across from her at the table, gazed at her with admiration. It was the third time Mr. Abbott had spoken sharply to Philip, urging him to eat. It was typical of Jenine to try to deflect the blame to herself, as well as to have found the time and space on the stove to have made popcorn for Philip just because she knew he liked it. Habitually thoughtful people were rare in Elizabeth's experience, particularly those as young as Jenine. Elizabeth herself had been contemplating throwing a spoon at her father-in-law. Chastened, she turned to excuse Philip from the table, but Mrs. Abbott intervened, saying tartly, "There will be no pie for those who don't eat their dinner."

Stephen turned to Philip confidingly. "It's peach," he whispered, "I saw it out in the kitchen." Philip sniffed, but picked up his fork. Elizabeth held her tongue.

Henry, seated at his mother's right, was methodically scraping up the last of his rice. In the silence that followed, the sound attracted Mr. Abbott's attention. "What was in that mess anyway," he demanded irritably, referring to the vegetarian meal Henry had, as always, prepared for himself.

"Brown rice, carrots, onion, broccoli, a bit of seaweed, some tofu," Henry said equably.

Mr. Abbott snorted and twisted sideways in his chair.

"What's tofu?" Stephen asked.

"You remember," Elizabeth said, "we had some not too long ago. It's textured protein made from soybeans."

"That white stuff?" Philip said. "It was yukky." There was still a good deal of food on his plate, cold now, and gluey. He made a face at it.

Mrs. Abbott turned to Henry. "You didn't cook up very much of that stuff, son," she said. "Are you sure you're getting enough protein? You have to have protein, you know, to stay healthy."

"I get more than enough protein, mother, thank you," Henry replied. "Protein doesn't mean just meat, you know; it's abundant in vegetables and grains, and in pulses like lentils and beans. It's practically impossible, in fact, for people in our society to eat too little protein. You have to try really hard."

"He's right, mum," Jenine said, getting up to clear the plates. "Vegetable protein is just as healthy, maybe even more so. And we could feed a lot more people at less cost if we used the land to plant soybeans instead of turning it over to cows."

Walter pulled a face. "Soybeans give me gas," he said.

"Not if they're cooked properly," Henry replied. "You have to rinse them several times."

Elizabeth, interested, leaned forward; Walter had complained that the soybean soup she'd made the week before had disagreed with him. "Before or after the cooking, Henry?"

"Both," he said.

"Boiled for how long?"

"An hour or so, if soaked overnight; five to six, if not."

Elizabeth shook her head. "It'll never sell," she said, "too much work. You can't expect American housewives to go to all that trouble when they can slap some chops on the grill, or pop a Lean Cuisine in the microwave."

Henry shrugged. "Whether or not I expect them to, I wish they would. And what makes you think the 'average housewife' can afford microwaves and Lean Cuisines?"

"They have them whether they can afford them or not," Mr. Abbott put in gruffly. "They just wave a credit card and there they are."

The remark, like so many of Mr. Abbott's, was followed by a silence. Elizabeth excused herself and joined Jenine in clearing the table. Philip's plate was still half-full; he was pushing his mashed potatoes around, trying to make the mound look smaller. "Shall I take it, Philip?" Jenine asked.

"Yes, do, for goodness' sake," Elizabeth answered, "all this fuss about eating is silly. If the child isn't hungry, he isn't hungry. But no pie, young man, and no hot dogs at the fireworks either, and next time don't take bigger helpings than you can manage." Philip grinned and slipped off his chair, escaping to the den.

The subject of vegetarianism, however, wasn't yet closed. When Henry went to the kitchen and returned with a cup of Inka, politely refusing a piece of his mother's pie, Mrs. Abbott abruptly banged the pie server down on the plate. "You'd think that at least on holidays you'd consent to eat our food," she said accusingly.

Henry looked at her in surprise. "I'm sorry, mother," he said mildly, "but as I've explained before, sugar isn't good for me. I haven't had an asthma attack in five years since changing the way I eat, and I'd rather not risk bringing them on again. If I've caused any trouble, I apologize; but for me what I eat means the difference between being sick and being well."

"Since when did you get a degree in medicine," Mr. Abbott cut in. "No doctor I know of ever recommended rice and seaweed and your whatchamacallit for asthma."

"I should think the proof was in the pudding, father, if you'll forgive the word play. In any case, why all the fuss? I'm only saying a vegetarian diet works for me; I'm not pushing it on anyone."

"Henry's right, Father Abbott," Elizabeth put in, "why is everyone picking on him? What earthly difference does it make what food one chooses to eat?"

"It makes a damned sight lot of difference," Mr. Abbott retorted. "People who eat beans do so because they can't afford to eat any better—like the Mexicans. Everybody needs meat: why else would they eat it every chance they get? Once they can afford meat they give up the beans. You think Mexicans are healthy? Baloney. And Mexicans aren't the point: they might not be able to eat well, but he can. Look at him, he's nothing but skin and bones. In my day people like that got TB. Nobody's got a right to throw away his life for some damn fool theory, that's what I believe."

Elizabeth lowered her eyes, embarrassed as always by her father-in-law's outbursts. Walter stiffened; Henry bowed his head. "But Henry is perfectly healthy, Daddy," Jenine soothed, removing his plate with one hand while touching his shoulder reassuringly with the other. "You don't have to be fat to be healthy, you know. Look at Gandhi: nobody could be thinner, and he was in his seventies when he died, wasn't he, and still walking miles every day. Henry's fine, and your pie was delicious, mum, when are you going to tell us your secret?"

Elizabeth stopped studying the tablecloth and joined in her praise. Jenine wasn't just being flattering or artfully changing the subject: Mrs. Abbott's pie crusts, made from scratch, were invariably perfect. Some of the peach juice had escaped near the fluted edges and hardened into a rich chewy syrup. It was so good Elizabeth was tempted to ask for seconds.

"Crisco," Mrs. Abbott said, sounding mollified. "You have to cut it in fine, so it's no bigger than field peas."

"I always thought you ate what you do not just because of your asthma but for moral reasons, Henry," Walter put in suddenly. "I'm surprised you haven't taken up the cause of Animal Rights yet, or have you? I hear it's the In thing these days."

Elizabeth stared at him, shocked that he should deliberately start baiting his brother when harmony of a kind had just been restored. It seemed purposely rude. In his own way, she thought, Walter had sulked through the meal as much as Philip. "Too bad the Orioles didn't win that game, we might all be in better moods," she said, but her comment was ignored.

"What's this animal rights business," Mr. Abbott growled. "They've got rights now too, have they?"

Henry swallowed the last of his Inka and placed his cup in the saucer. "One right at least, yes," he said calmly, addressing his father, "the right not to suffer unnecessary pain."

Walter was toying with his silverware, aligning his fork so that it was perfectly parallel to his knife. "Unnecessary as defined by whom," he asked coolly, "us or them?"

"By us, obviously: we are their caretakers. By the way," Henry added, his tone this time matching his brother's in provocativeness, "I assume the weapons you are working on over at Edgewood are tested on animals first. Do the experiments take place there, in the labs, or do you contract out that part?"

Walter smiled coldly. "You know such information is classified," he said. "You know I can't answer."

"What's 'Classified'?" Stephen interjected.

"Government secrets," Mrs. Abbott said, "things we can't talk about because the Russians might hear."

Elizabeth giggled. "We're all North Americans here," she said, which drew from Walter a contemptuous glance, as if the remark was beneath her.

"That's true," Jenine put in, "but we're not all adults."

Mrs. Abbott pushed her chair back with a decided thump. "You'd think this family could get together once or twice a year without fighting," she said tearfully. "We have differences, I know, but why we just don't let them go at that is beyond me."

Immediately Mr. Abbott was contrite. "You boys apologize to your mother," he ordered, without, Elizabeth noticed, offering any apology himself. Henry stood up and gathered his mother in a hug. "Just because I don't eat your pie doesn't mean I don't love you, mom," he said, "and just because this family argues doesn't mean we don't love each other. We do, really we do."

His mother, freeing herself from his arms, refused to smile. "You should find better ways of showing it then," she said flatly, after which she excused herself and went upstairs to her room.

*   *   *   *

The stairs were difficult but she managed, though nearing the top she had to rest on every second one. She closed the bedroom door and sank into the bed, pulling her afghan around her. She was exhausted, each nerve-end of her skin tingling with irritation. A jangle of nerves, her mother used to say of herself, and that's what she was now, a jangle of nerves, her mind buzzing ceaselessly with worries, about Walter and Henry, and above everything else, about her health. She could detect no sign of the progress the doctor had promised her after the hysterectomy; she had had the operation five months ago and still she wasn't on her feet, or if she was, like today, it was because she had been jerked there and held upright by puppet strings. The mother puppet, the wife puppet, the grandmother puppet, jerked to her feet by others' needs. When the strings were loosed, she collapsed.

The afghan she had pulled over her shoulders was one she had crocheted years ago, when Walter was in college. It was faded now, and smelled of something she couldn't place, like Vaseline, or some kind of hair oil. It needed washing. So many things needed doing that she didn't have the energy for and couldn't ask John to do, and couldn't ask anyone else to do. They said Mr. Evans at the church did odd jobs, but she couldn't ask him to wash her afghan, or do much else. It would embarrass John and make him even more difficult....

Why wasn't she getting better, why did she have so little energy? There was something more the matter with her than recovering from that operation; those strange piercing pains in her abdomen had returned. They were more frequent now, as well as more intense. At first she had tried to dismiss them, but when they didn't go away she had made an appointment at the church to talk to Reverend James.

She had told him about the pains once before, years and years ago right after Sylvie died, which is when they started. The first one had come when the policeman told her at the door that Sylvie was dead, that a drunk had slammed into her car and killed her. The man's words had stabbed her like an ice pick; she had doubled over with a sudden pain in her abdomen and had to sit down. The spasms of pain had gone on like that for years, always coming unexpectedly, though usually months apart. She had had her gall bladder removed on the advice of her doctor; the pains subsided for a while, though the thought of Sylvie, for years afterward, would still sometimes provoke an echo of that first sharp jab.

Not always, however, not every time she thought of her. Sometimes she'd take out the photograph album she and Sylvie had put together when she was sixteen and look at the pictures and remember the happy times and forgive Sylvie for dying. Though she would never forgive the drunk who killed her.

Killed us, she corrected. For in her view he had killed them both. She had carried on all these years (she had had to, there were all those mother and now grandmother strings), but it had not seemed real. In reality, she felt, she had died; she had stopped living the moment she opened that door and saw that policeman standing there with his cap in his hands. She had kept on walking and moving around, but it was mostly pretense.

Pretending took too much energy; she was tired of it. What did it all amount to anyway? She and John had raised three children with all the love and care they could muster; as parents they had done as well as they knew how, and look at the result. One child dead and two others who did nothing but fight. She hated the way Walter made his living, and she hated Henry for showing him up; and for being the town's laughingstock, and lonely, and poor.

She could feel tears coming, but she was too tired to reach for a tissue. All she had ever wanted was for the family to have come out right, like a perfect pie fresh from the oven. She didn't know what she had done wrong, and no matter how many times she had asked the Lord He hadn't given her an answer. It was His will, Reverend James said, reminding her that the rain fell on the just and the unjust alike. That was so, but in her heart she could not accept it. She couldn't help wanting things to come out right, and grieving that they hadn't. She was tired of praying that they would, tired of hope.

Another twinge of pain prompted her to reach for the tiny white pills on her bedside table. No more than two, the doctor had said, and only at bedtime. It wasn't bedtime yet, was it? Probably not, but she would have to pretend it was. Bedtime was when you were this tired. She was a grownup now, she thought defiantly, she could sleep whenever she wanted to.

She curled her knees up to her chest, which helped relieve the pain in her abdomen. However else God had arranged things, He had at least given man sleep.

CHAPTER 4

▼

"I want to stay here too, the real fireworks will be on TV," Philip complained when Jenine told him his grandmother was too tired to be going with them. This annoyed Walter. "What's real is what's in front of you," he told Philip sharply, "not something that appears on a screen." He was beginning to seriously dislike Philip's constant preference for television-mediated experience, as well as his assumption that the local fireworks display wasn't worth watching if it didn't measure up to Washington's extravagance.

"Your grandmother is staying home because she's not well, Philip, she's not staying to watch TV," Elizabeth reminded him. "Come, get in the car, you'll like it when you're there."

The park was only ten minutes from the farmhouse. Walter drove, his father beside him in the front, Jenine and Elizabeth in the middle seats, Stephen and Philip in the back. It was too short a trip for the boys to play either the cow game or Road Signs. There was nothing to do but look out the windows, which were rolled all the way down. The heat was still stifling.

"Ugh," Philip said, wrinkling his nose. "What's that smell?"

"Cow manure," Elizabeth answered.

Stephen suppressed a giggle: if his grandfather hadn't been in the car she would have said "cow shit."

"It stinks," Philip repeated.

"Yes, but it's what makes things grow."

Mr. Abbott turned around in his seat. "I imagine there are better topics of conversation for the Fourth of July than animal waste," he said sternly.

He might as well have commanded silence. What were they supposed to talk about, Philip thought resentfully, George Washington? He resumed looking out the window.

Stephen put his hand in his pocket, fingering the stones Henry had given him. On impulse he took them out and showed them to Philip, but the light in the car kept shifting and Philip, unimpressed, said that stones were boring. Stung, Stephen, put them back in his pocket.

Some day he'd find a stone that had magic powers and then Philip would be sorry, he thought to himself. Better yet, he'd find a stone with the power to make his brother disappear. He hunched down and glared out the window.

Elizabeth, looking out the opposite side, was absorbed in the spectacle of the changing light. The sun had just dipped below the horizon and the air was trembling with a soft, lustrous tone. No matter how many times she had experienced southern twilights they never failed to induce in her a mood of wonder. They seemed magical, even mystical, like the glints of fire that flashed from deep inside certain gemstones. The light kept deepening, intensifying the blue and green of trees and grass and sky, making you feel as if you'd never seen blue or green before. It was so beautiful she wanted to cry, or else giggle at its excessive romanticism. The sultry air was drenched with the heavy scent of honeysuckle, as far as she was concerned the most erotic fragrance in the world. She shivered slightly, thinking of Henry and what had passed between them that afternoon. How serious he had been, how "heavy," as they used to say: she was grateful he had elected to stay behind with Mrs. Abbott, in case he was needed.

When they pulled into the parking lot the first fireflies were out. Stephen and Philip chased a few, then lit their sparklers and ran down the path to the riverbank, spraying silver sparks in all directions. Walter unloaded the picnic basket and caught Elizabeth up.

He couldn't help noticing how delectable she looked. She was wearing a pale green skirt and a crisp white halter top, her only ornament a sea-green stone on a golden chain that hung between her breasts. The colors set off her tan, and her tawny blonde hair. The thought of making love to her later excited him; for reasons he didn't care to analyze he especially enjoyed fucking in his parents' house. He was disappointed when he put his arm around her waist and she shied away.

"What's wrong?" he asked, "did I do something?"

"Of course not, don't be silly," she said.

In fact she moved away because she suddenly remembered, to her astonishment, that she had forgotten to remove Henry's diary from the pocket of her skirt. Fortunately it was in the right-hand pocket and not the left, or Walter would have felt it when he pulled her toward him. The fact that it had slipped her mind had shocked her.

Her denial that Walter had done anything offensive was also not true. In her view, he had been unforgivably rude to Henry all evening, behaving like a spiteful child. She despised him when he acted that way: it made her look down on him, which she hated. It was also a sexual turn-off; how could you be aroused by someone who behaved like a child? It turned sex into something vaguely revolting, something with a perverse, semi-incestuous taint.

"I do think it was rather stupid of you at dinner to try to pick a quarrel like that with Henry," she said, keeping a careful space between them as they walked.

He resented her tone, but he judged it impolitic to argue. "You're right," he conceded, "though it seemed to me my dear brother was being a bit provocative himself. However, *mea culpa*: it was foolish. Am I forgiven?"

Again he put his hand on her waist and tried to draw her towards him. The gesture struck her as proprietary. She suffered it, but when he went farther and tried to nuzzle the nape of her neck she slid away.

At the riverbank Jenine had spread a blanket beneath a willow tree. Elizabeth sat down and opened the picnic basket. Walter and Mr. Abbott joined them, while the boys grabbed their sparklers and ran off to the riverbank, where the other children were. It was almost dark now; you couldn't see much but the dancing lights of sparklers on both sides of the river. Elizabeth sat back on her heels and watched, enchanted. It was as if the children were communicating with each other in a private language, signaling back and forth. Their movements seemed choreographed: one side would initiate a pattern and the other would repeat it, with variations. They would move their arms in slow circles, or sway from side to side in imitation of trees. They kept it up until the first preliminary rocket set off a shower of pink sparks in the sky, announcing the beginning of the show.

The performance lasted for fifteen minutes. "Aren't they wonderful," Jenine breathed, after she and Elizabeth had exclaimed together several times in succession. She'd always loved fireworks, she said shyly, they had seemed to her miraculous as a child; and still did. On impulse, Elizabeth reached over and squeezed her hand, as a series of Roman candles exploded in the sky, sending out multiple golden fountains. Each detonation made Mr. Abbott jump and let out a peculiar noise. Jenine and Elizabeth smothered their giggles behind their hands. The spectacle seemed to go on and on, uniting in the darkness people of all races and ages and degrees of wealth, as it was meant to do. Finally there was a lull, a period of suspense when they stared at the blue-gray wreaths of smoke hanging in the air.

They held their breaths, until, as always, a final cascade of red white and blue brought everyone to their feet.

The lights came on in the park and the band in the bandstand played America The Beautiful, followed more energetically by The Stars and Stripes Forever. Philip came back to the blanket, Stephen trailing behind. "Can we go to the concession for something to drink?" he asked. "Stephen's thirsty."

"There's Pepsi in the cooler, Philip," Walter objected.

"But it's not cold. It's been in there all day, and the cold-pack thing's not cold any more. Please can we go? I promise I won't buy anything but a drink."

Elizabeth, with a sigh, reached for her purse. Walter turned on her sharply. "I haven't given him permission yet that I know of," he snapped. "If his grandfather and I can drink warm beer, I don't see why they can't make do with less than ice-cold Pepsi."

"For pity's sake, Walter," Elizabeth said, "why make a thing of it? If you want a cold beer, go buy one."

"Please say we can go, Dad," Stephen put in, "I ate my supper, and Philip's promised."

Walter gave it up. "Come back when the band is finished," he said curtly.

Mr. Abbott shook his head, but accepted the beer Walter offered him.

*   *   *   *

Philip and Stephen raced off, not realizing until they got to the concession stand that they had only a dollar between them. Philip wanted a hot dog as well as a coke, but he knew it would look suspicious if he went back for more money so he proposed, as a "compromise," that they sell one of Stephen's stones. You could sell people anything, he said, if you made them feel sorry for you. "We could say our parents gave us the money for a hot dog and we lost it. I don't think we should have to be asking our parents for money all the time if we can make it on our own," he told Stephen in his grown-up voice. "I bet we could sell them to lots of people. They're pretty. Women could put them on chains and make necklaces of them, like Mom does. We could sell them for a dollar each."

"I thought you said my stones were boring," Stephen said, looking at him suspiciously.

"So maybe we'd get fifty cents then, that's all we need. Come on, let's see what you got."

Reluctantly Stephen pulled the stones from his pocket. If it was only a matter of one, it might be all right.

"That one's the best," Philip said, "it's the smoothest."

He was pointing at the speckled brown and white oval, which happened to be Stephen's favorite. It was the perfect size, and he'd grown used to the feel of it against his palm. "Not that one," he objected.

"Well, pick whatever one you want then, it doesn't matter. They'll give us the money because we're kids, and it's the Fourth of July."

Stephen hung back. "What if they turn us down?" he asked.

Philip shrugged. "Then we'll try somebody else."

As it turned out, it wasn't difficult. In fact, the first woman they offered the stones to took pity on them and without asking any questions gave them a dollar. She chose the gray and white one, exclaiming about it in admiring tones that sounded to Stephen put on. Philip thanked her and went immediately to the stand to buy a hot dog and a Pepsi, which they shared, trading bites and sips. When they were finished, they divided the ice from the paper cup and wandered around the park looking at people.

In the car on the way home everyone was subdued. Elizabeth turned the radio to the classical music station, which was playing piano music of some sort, Mozart it sounded like. It deepened Stephen's feeling that he was going to be sick. His half of the hot dog had become an indigestible lump in his stomach. To comfort himself, he put his hand in his pocket and fingered the remaining three stones.

The thought of the missing one weighed on him. It was strange to think that it had been changed into paper money which was then changed into food which had then become a lump in his stomach. It was as if he had eaten the stone, in a roundabout way.

He shouldn't have let Philip talk him into selling it. It wasn't right, he thought, and the proof was his stomach ache. Henry had found the stone and given it to him as a gift, and when he did that, it became personal, not just a stone. It wasn't right to sell personal things, you should only give them. The woman who bought it probably wouldn't even wear it, she'd probably throw it away.

The idea made him miserable, and his misery made him defensive. It was Philip's fault, he thought. Philip had tricked him, he was always tricking him. Why, he wondered, and why did he, Stephen, keep letting it happen? He vowed on the remaining stones never to let Philip talk him into anything again.

＊   ＊   ＊   ＊

When they reached the house, it was dark. Mrs. Abbott was asleep upstairs, and Henry too had apparently gone to bed. Elizabeth supervised the children into their pajamas and made up the sofa-bed in the den. The boys, obviously tired, lay down without a murmur; for once she believed them when they promised to leave the television alone. Saying good night to Jenine and her father-in-law, she went upstairs.

Walter followed close behind her. As she opened the bedroom door she felt him slip his hand around her waist. She wriggled away, but with a smile which offered promise. "I left my overnight case in the hall," she said, "would you mind going down and getting it?"

When she heard his footsteps on the stairs, she went into the bathroom and concealed Henry's diary beneath a stack of towels at the bottom of the linen closet. She was undressing in the bedroom when Walter returned. "Mmm," he murmured as she slipped into her nightgown, "you are a delectable sight still, madame."

Elizabeth, slipping into bed, started to reply but thought better of it. Walter undressed and took his place beside her, reaching for her without bothering to turn out the light.

At his parents' house, she knew, he liked to make love with the light on, as if it were somehow daring. Lately he had taken up the practice of licking her body from her neck to her toes as part of an elaborate foreplay performance. It was designed to turn her on, but unfortunately it more often had the opposite effect, making her see herself either as an inanimate object or as a goddess he was paying ritual homage to, both of which made her uncomfortable. She preferred making love when it was face to face: personal, mutual. She gently urged him on, feigning arousal. When he finally entered her she relaxed and let him proceed at his own pace, but eventually she grew impatient. She urged him in ways she knew excited him, and he came quickly.

Afterwards she rather despised herself for her hypocrisy, and irritated at him for being so easily taken in. It reinforced her sense that he made love to her only for his own gratification, no matter how much attention he officially paid to her erogenous zones. He was play-acting, even if he didn't know it.

When she knew from his breathing that he was deeply asleep (he had a knack of dropping like a stone into sleep two or three minutes after sex), she slipped out of bed and quietly put on her robe. Turning off the light, she tiptoed into the bathroom, where she locked the door and filled the tub with warm water, placing a facecloth over the stopper in the drain to muffle the sound. Then she retrieved Henry's diary from beneath the towels.

The tub was a harsh, ugly green, but it fit the curve of her back comfortably, not like some of those modern square-backed horrors designed by men who obviously preferred showers. She sprinkled the water with the bath salts Mrs. Abbott had thoughtfully placed beside the soap dish and relaxed, letting her arms half float. It was a luxury to be alone.

That making love to Walter didn't always result in her having an orgasm had long ago ceased to bother her. She still more or less enjoyed it, though increasingly it had come to seem a bit like a duty—not an onerous duty, and certainly not a self-sacrificing one, but a responsibility, a prudent act on her part if she wanted to keep their life running smoothly. She had learned years ago that it was less trouble to make love to Walter than to put up with his irritability when she refused. The way she looked at it, sex for men seemed to have greater importance than it did for women; their ego-identity was more tied up with it, and since it was no skin off her back to keep Walter happy, she didn't see why she should refuse. It wasn't as if their lovemaking was painful, or even a pain in the neck; in fact, she enjoyed pleasing, and one thing she could say for Walter was that he was genuinely appreciative.

She remembered a friend of hers surprising her once by saying of men, "Poor things, fucking is the only way they know to show their love," a statement that had struck her as shockingly condescending but oddly true. Curious to think that a stray remark like that could benefit someone years later though, that Walter should profit from a comment made by someone he had never known.

She reached for a towel and dried her hands, then carefully picked up the black ringed notebook from the floor beside her. The lines on the pages were very close together, and were covered completely with Henry's small, neat script. It was pretty writing, almost feminine, done with a fine-lined black pen. She leafed through the pages. From the dates she gathered he wrote in it once or twice a week, sometimes at length, sometimes in snippets. The entries began on January 1 and ended that afternoon, on July 4, 1986.

At the back of the notebook, folded in half, was a leaflet of his which she had never seen. Before examining the diary, she read it through.

STRAIGHT TALK ABOUT BIGEYE

Dear Friends,

As you know, the U.S. Congress has recently agreed to proceed with the production of the binary chemical weapon known as the Bigeye bomb, for deployment in England and West Germany. The Pentagon argues (a) that the deployment of this weapon is safer than the old "unitary" chemical weapons it will replace; (b) that it will strengthen nuclear deterrence by serving as an intermediate weapons system that could be used in event of war; and (c) that it will strengthen deterrence generally and help keep the peace in Europe. It is our belief that all of these arguments are false.

The current U.S. chemical arsenal amounts to over 40,000 short tonnes of nerve and mustard gas, containing enough lethal doses to kill the entire world's population 5,000 times over. Over half of this is in bulk storage, but 15% of it fills some 800,000 modern artillery shells and 13,000 bombs. The current stockpile of unitary munitions, old as they are, actually constitutes a more credible deterrent than binaries.

The entire binary program, including disposing of the existing chemical stockpile it is designed to replace, may cost $20 billion or more, and is not without significant risks of its own. The Pentagon plans to produce 1,200,000 binary 155-mm. artillery rounds and 44,000 Bigeye bombs. Also being developed are binary eight-inch howitzer shells and binary warheads for the "multiple-launch rocket system," for air-to-ground missiles and for Pershing II and Cruise missiles.

BIGEYE: DETERRENT OR 'INTER-MEDIATE WEAPON'?

The Pentagon alternates between saying that it wants Bigeye as a deterrent (implying that it will never be used) and claiming that it is an "intermediate weapon," i.e., that America could introduce chemical weapons in an attack situation and thus "reduce the chance of escalation to nuclear war." But would this reduce the chance or increase it? And what would happen to the civilian population if chemical weapons were used? Do you know?

The facts are these. According to the Pentagon's own studies, most of the victims of a chemical attack would be civilians. It is estimated that twenty to one hundred civilians will die for every soldier who succumbs, since only military personnel will be equipped with protective clothing and gas masks. Everyone and everything within an area of 30,000 square miles would be lethally contaminated. A full-scale chemical exchange could result in as many as eighty million deaths. The consequences to the region's ecosystem—the biological life-support system of the people who remain—would be equally catastrophic.

Binary chemical weapons are profoundly destabilizing. Not only will they encourage chemical proliferation in other countries (since our own program gives them the Superpower Seal of Approval), but they will weaken rather than strengthen deterrence, making escalation to nuclear war more rather than less likely. The reasons for this are:

1. The US has said it will not deploy binaries in continental Europe except during a crisis. But such an act would be highly destabilizing in a crisis. It could be read as preparation for offensive warfare, thereby actually encouraging rather than deterring Soviet first-use of either chemical or nuclear weapons.

2. Chemical weapons are inherently escalatory; they might hasten the crossing of the firebreak between chemical and nuclear war. Since they are indiscriminate weapons of mass destruction, their use signals a willingness to use extreme measures to achieve political ends. It is a relatively short escalatory step from there to breaching the nuclear barrier, just as it seemed a small step at the end of the last war to move from the firebombing of Dresden and Tokyo to the atomic bombings of Hiroshima and Nagasaki.

One of the few positive gains from World War I was the Geneva Convention outlawing chemical warfare. The U.S.A. is a full signatory to this agreement.

WE BELIEVE THE PRODUCTION OF CHEMICAL WEAPONS MUST BE ABOLISHED WORLD-WIDE

Chemical weapons are an immoral, redundant weapons system which do nothing to enhance our security. Instead they add a further threat to the continued existence of life on this planet. Please join our efforts to make this a safer world. PEACE IS EVERYBODY'S BUSINESS.

On the back of the flyer were footnotes, a bibliography of suggested reading, and an address for a subscription to Year One, the newsletter put out by a group called Jonah House in Baltimore. There was also the address of Disarmament Action, which Elizabeth presumed was Henry's own "group," though according to Walter, there was no one else in it but him.

She replaced the flyer in the diary and set it beside her on the floor. Then she slipped deeper into the water, letting it came up to her chin. Sometimes the world was too crazy, and too scary, to think about. Henry's arguments seemed to her unanswerable; they were simply common sense. Or maybe she wasn't competent to answer them, she didn't know; she supposed Walter could, but he'd treat the whole question as a debate to score points about. He wouldn't engage the issue emotionally, he wouldn't try to see eighty million people dead in their homes, or even eighty.

She closed her eyes. It was so obviously futile, what Henry was doing. He was right, of course he was right, but what was the point? He'd never change the minds of the military, no matter if he stood out there at the gates for a hundred years. For to the military, it was equally obvious that the more weapons you had the stronger you were, and the stronger you were, the safer you were: nothing would ever shake that "logic." As to the American people, they seemed to her ignorant and indifferent in equal measure, swallowing without question what their media fed them, their civic duty fulfilled by pulling a lever in a polling booth every four years and waving their flags on the Fourth of July.

She picked up the soap and soaped her hands. A sudden impulse made her shape her thumbs and forefingers into an O, like she used to in the bathtub as a child; if you blew on the soapy film between your fingers, gently enough and persistently enough, fat bubbles formed and wafted out into the air. She blew three in a row, to distract herself. For how was she different from the average American? Even though she hadn't even been born in this country, she was just as susceptible to its patriotism: when they had splattered the sky tonight with red white and blue and the band played America The Beautiful she had felt tears come to her eyes. She wanted to believe in her adopted country, as much as anyone born here. There was a great reservoir of longing in America to believe in the myth that the country's leaders were honest and wise, and intended nothing but good for the world. And there stood Henry, saying No, look what is happening, Grandfather Ronnie is spending your tax money on nerve gas, with bipartisan approval. How did this fit together with America The Beautiful?

It seemed to her the myth was wearing thinner every year. If Americans were genuinely doing good around the world, how could they possibly be so unpopular there, why did American young people feel safer traveling with Canadian flags stitched on their knapsacks? Surely the overseas image of the U.S. wasn't all the result of communist propaganda. She had asked Walter once why he thought Americans were despised in Europe and detested in Latin America, and he had answered that they were both jealous. The remark had struck her as arrogant, but it had enough truth in it that she hadn't argued.

She picked up the sponge and soaped her arms, thinking how depressing it all was. How had their lives come to this, how had hers? Here she was sitting in a bathtub secretly reading her radical brother-in-law's diary, for which she should be feeling guilty, but instead she was angry, angry at Walter for making things for the government that shouldn't be made, angry at herself for her acquiescence in his job, most of all angry at the United States of America for being so sickened by greed and fear it had turned into a country impossible to live in with any conscience. Last but not least, angry at Henry, for being too stupid to see that there was no way to change anything, that it was too late, the ball game already over. What would happen was not in their hands—either millions would die in some horrible war or they wouldn't, and no amount of witnessing at the gates would change the outcome. Henry was an anachronism, a Don Quixote; he should have lived in the days of Tom Paine, when people could be stirred to action by pamphlets called Common Sense.

She wondered if Henry had sent copies of his writings to the press. Of course he must have, and of course they would not have been printed.

She got out and dried herself and put on her nightgown and robe. Then, sitting on the fuzzy pink cover of Mrs. Abbott's toilet, she opened the diary and began skimming through it.

Much of it seemed to be commentary on news items of the day—-the Challenger disaster, the struggle in Central America, the level of funding for Star Wars. She scanned the pages for more personal entries. The first to catch her eye was the mention of a wet dream, in his entry of February 18.

"I dreamed last night I was floating in a clear blue body of water, as if I was in a secret cave or the quarry where Walter and I used to swim when we were kids. I was naked, awash in bliss, the sky arching over me. The thought came to me that I was "in the embrace of the divine." When I was awakened by the cold stickiness of sperm on the sheets, I didn't know whether to laugh or cry.

This hasn't happened in a long time. The sap readying itself for spring.

Elizabeth shivered. Had Henry wanted her to read such things, or had he forgotten he had written them? "It might help her to know him better," he had said of the diary: is this what he meant? The language of this entry seemed different from the others, more sensual, obviously, but also more poetic. Still, she was struck by how chastely platonic the dream was, considering, and how he had omitted the actual orgasm experience, as if out of modesty. *In the embrace of the divine*: even his sex, she reflected, was suffused with religion, a disembodied transcendental yearning. Poor Henry: it must be hard to be single and burdened with so many scruples.

She closed the notebook. She would read it thoroughly, later; it would be a secret pleasure to look forward to when they were home. She felt too furtive reading it here.

She switched off the light and stepped out into the bedroom, feeling for the edge of the rug with her toes. Silently she slid the notebook into her overnight case, which she had left open on the desk. Then she carefully entered the bed. Walter stirred slightly and made a snorting sound, but turned over and continued sleeping.

She lay back on her pillow, suddenly very tired. Sleep wouldn't come easily though, there were too many new things to think about. She should try to empty her mind, concentrate on her breathing, remind herself that Henry's wet dreams were no concern of hers. But she couldn't help thinking of his loneliness, and her own, and of every human being who was aware that their sacred planet home could be annihilated at any moment by impious men, and she couldn't prevent tears from seeping beneath her lids, making wet spots on the pillow.

CHAPTER 5

▼

On the way home from church, Stephen sat in the back seat of the station wagon and tried to figure it all out. Church was for him a rare experience: he could remember only a few other times he'd been taken there. Once was when they had visited his Canadian grandmother in Ontario; hers had been a Unitarian church, and the service was held in an ordinary building. At least, that's how he remembered it. The church that his Maryland grandparents went to was called St. John's Presbyterian. It was a white wooden building with a pointed roof and a steeple at the top. Outside there was a glassed-in bulletin board with white letters on a black background telling you the time of the service and what the sermon was.

The sermon today had been on "God's Forgiveness." Stephen hadn't heard much of it: he'd been distracted at the very beginning when the minister asked them to all rise and recite The Apostles' Creed. It was printed at the end of the hymn books, which were in racks on the backs of the pews. Walter handed out three of them, opened at the right page. Everyone in the church recited it in unison. His father, Stephen noticed, didn't need to read it from the book, apparently knowing it from memory. His Uncle Henry and his grandparents knew it too, but his mother and Philip had had to read it. Aunt Jenine rose with the others, but she neither read nor recited it; instead she stood with her eyes closed and listened. Stephen supposed that was because she was Catholic and this was a Protestant church. Catholics weren't supposed to go to any church other than their own, but Jenine said that this was a special exception; since it was a family occasion, God wouldn't mind.

Stephen didn't understand the whole business of Catholics and Protestants. While the sermon was going on, he concentrated on reading and rereading the Apostles' Creed as a memory exercise. He liked memorizing things; it was nice to have them in your head for nowhere times like when you were standing in line in the school cafeteria, or waiting at your seat for the others to finish their tests and the papers to be collected. He liked the poems they were made to memorize in school. "Barbara Fritchie" was his favorite this year; he would recite it to himself on particularly cold mornings when he delivered *The Baltimore Sun* on his paper route. He also liked "Thanatopsis," though he didn't understand it as well.

In the car he tried going over the Apostles' Creed to see how much he had retained. "I believe in God the Father, maker of heaven and earth, and of Jesus Christ his only Son our Lord." The rhythms made that part easy; the rest was more like prose. "He was conceived of the Holy Ghost, suffered under Pontius Pilate, was crucified dead and buried. On the third day he rose from the dead and sitteth on the right hand of God the Father Almighty, from whence he shall come to judge the quick and the dead."

He paused. What did "the quick and the dead" mean? He should make note of the parts he didn't understand and ask about them later, he thought. But then he found he couldn't remember the rest of the Creed, which was always the way when you distracted yourself by thinking about the meaning of individual words. The trick was to just go with the rhythms and not worry about the meaning.

He began again, and this time he was able to remember it all the way through. "I believe in the Holy Ghost, the Holy Christian Church, the communion of saints, the forgiveness of sins, the resurrection of the body and the life everlasting, Amen." "Amen" was what you said at the end of things, like at the end of a prayer.

No one in the car was saying much. His mother had turned on the radio to some violin music. Jenine and Uncle Henry and Mrs. Abbott were in the middle seat, his grandfather in the back with him and Philip. Stephen leaned forward and tapped his aunt on the shoulder. "Aunt Jenine, what's an Apostle?" he asked.

Jenine turned around in surprise. "The Apostles were the twelve disciples of Christ who set out to preach the gospel," she said. "Why?"

"I was practicing learning The Apostles' Creed so I could say it next time without looking at the book," Stephen said.

His grandfather patted him approvingly on the knee. "Good boy," he said.

"What does *creed* mean?"

"It means what you believe. The word comes from the Latin '*credo*,' which means 'I believe.' The Apostles' Creed is a summary of what Christians believe."

"Oh." Stephen mentally went over the things they were supposed to believe to see if he understood them all. "What's the quick and the dead then?"

Again Jenine answered simply. "*Quick* is the old-fashioned word for alive. It means Christ will come to judge both the people who are living and the people who have died."

"Is there a special time for him to come or could it just be any time," Stephen asked, "like right now, while we're driving home?" The possibility had never occurred to him.

"Damn right," his grandfather growled. "He could come five minutes from now, or any time He wants."

Stephen looked at him, dubious. The idea was so bizarre it shut him up for a minute, but then he decided that that was just his grandfather's way of thinking. Stephen didn't really trust his grandfather's answers, not like he trusted Jenine's or Uncle Henry's.

He leaned forward again, to make clear that his next question was for the seat in front of him. "What's the communion of saints?" he asked.

"That refers to Heaven," Jenine said. "It means you believe in Heaven."

Stephen looked out the window. Unlike her other answers, this one led to a lot more questions, like what saints were really and whether you only got to Heaven if you were one, and why they didn't just say "I believe in Heaven" to begin with, instead of believing in "the communion of the saints." But since he knew it wasn't polite to ask so many questions, he decided on just one more. "I don't understand the 'resurrection of the body' either," he said. "What does that mean?"

Henry chuckled. "Let's hear you on that one, Jenine," he teased.

Mrs. Abbott interrupted. "It means that when Christ our Lord comes to judge the quick and dead, all the dead will rise up from their graves, and that will be that," she said with finality. "Now let's hear no more about it, Stephen, it will lead to an argument for sure."

Stephen retreated in consternation. "People believe different things about God and the Bible, Stephen," Jenine said gently when she saw his expression. "They interpret certain passages differently, and this sometimes leads to arguments. It's better to talk about things we all agree on, don't you think? We're all Christians, and that's what matters."

"But how do I know what everybody agrees on if we're not allowed to talk about it?" he protested.

Mr. Abbott turned sideways, raising his shoulders so that he looked bigger than when he was leaning back. "These are questions you should be asking your Sunday School teacher," he said sternly.

Stephen didn't answer. He and Philip had never been to Sunday school, and his grandfather knew it.

"Your grandfather is right," Elizabeth put in, turning down the radio. "You should learn all about Christianity if you're interested in it. Would you like to start going to Sunday school?"

Stephen shrank in his seat. More school wasn't what he had in mind; he didn't much care for school. He preferred the holidays when he could do as he liked, but he was conscious that both his grandparents were looking at him expectantly. "Yeah, sure, some time," he mumbled.

"Growing up like savages," his grandfather growled. "Worst thing that ever happened to this country was taking prayer out of the schools. They should be made to read the Bible every morning, like we were."

"Why?" Walter said, turning the radio off. "He can read it himself any time he wants to. You gave him a copy last Christmas, remember?"

Stephen squirmed, sorry he had started this subject. His grandfather's next question was sure to be if he had read it yet, which of course he hadn't. The print was too small, and the language too old-fashioned. Fortunately his grandmother gave his grandfather one of her warning looks, and he made do with a sniff.

"Who were the twelve Apostles anyway, Jenine?" Henry asked, "I've forgotten. John, Peter, and Matthew, Mark and Luke, but who were the others?"

Walter snorted. "We'll be listing the Seven Deadly Sins next, for god's sake. Or the Seven Dwarfs."

"I know those," Philip said. "Grumpy, Sneezy, Bashful, Sleepy, Happy and Doc."

"That's only six," Stephen pointed out, "you left one out."

"Snoopy," Henry said, and everyone laughed.

"One of the Apostles was named Stephen, you know," Jenine put in. "Have you never heard of Saint Stephen?"

"No, he hasn't," Walter said sharply. "We don't *do* saints."

"But was that who I was named after?" Stephen asked.

Elizabeth tried to turn around all the way but her seat belt wouldn't let her. "You weren't named after anybody that I know of, Stephen, I just liked the name," she said. Actually, she thought, she had probably named him after Joyce's Stephen Daedalus, so he was named after a saint of sorts. She had been studying the novel the year before he was born.

"I remember," Philip said as they pulled into the drive. "It wasn't Snoopy, it was Dopey."

"Whew," Henry breathed. "I'm glad that's settled."

Jenine looked at him and smiled.

*   *   *   *

But of course nothing was ever really settled in this family, Elizabeth thought later when they were back on the highway, certainly not issues of faith. The various shades of religion among the Abbotts had always been an object of curiosity to her, ranging from Mr. Abbott's "Huntley Street" fundamentalism to Henry's quasi-mystical pacifism to Walter's contemptuous atheism, in addition to Jenine's quiet devotion to the Catholic Church and Mrs. Abbott's dutiful Protestantism, the kind that emphasized good works like bake sales, and visits to the sick. She supposed she should include in the inventory her own pale shade of religiosity, a sort of nebulous, post-Aquarian Age quivering, more a longing for faith than the thing itself.

As far as she could tell, Walter never felt a need for religion, and certainly never longed for it or mourned its absence. She didn't know whether this was something she admired or despised in him.

The picnic that afternoon, ham sandwiches, potato salad, and pie, was held in the backyard, under the trees. Perhaps because it was outside, or because they were subdued by the experience of going to church, but everyone managed to stay civil. The boys seemed listless, and were easily persuaded to get back into the car after the food was cleared away and the good-byes said. Driving home, there was another ball game on the radio, which this time Elizabeth didn't protest. She gave Stephen her traveling pillow, and he soon dozed off. Philip was happily absorbed in the game. She was free to think her own thoughts.

This usually meant sorting out, her feelings, or trying to. Prominent among these, at the moment, was fear, or rather, an undertow of dread when she thought of reading Henry's diary. She was aware of being drawn into something, something she knew she should resist but also knew she wouldn't. This wasn't the first time she had found herself sinking into a passive, fatalistic state of mind: the sensation was familiar, the sense that you were nearing a cliff top, that a few more steps and you'd likely slide over the edge into something forbidden, perhaps even fatal. But it was already too late to change course, or so you rationalized, for inside the passivity, driving it, there was a powerful curiosity to know what would happen if you abandoned herself, took the line of least resistance and allowed yourself to be pulled into whatever lay on the other side of the cliff. How otherwise would she know how far she would slide? If she held back, she might spend the rest of her life wondering.

This will-less lethargy had taken hold of her at least twice before in her life, once with one of her first lovers, and again when she first started sleeping with Walter. The first was a disaster, the second resulted in Phillip's conception, and marriage. She wondered if she possessed a self-destructive streak, if she was subject to recurring spells of somnambulism? For she *was* in that place again, the space before action, the promontory where theoretically you were still free to choose one path or another, though by then the idea of choice had become ambiguous. Of course she was "free," technically: she could choose, for example, to return the diary unread. But she knew she wouldn't.

Elizabeth had always had trouble believing in free will. The first American prose work they had read in her Survey of American Literature class had gone straight to her heart—Jonathan Edwards' hoary old sermon, "Sinners In The Hands Of An Angry God." It was a meditation on the text, *Their foot shall slide in due time,* a line whose uncompromising finality she found inexplicably thrilling. Even the idea that it was "*their foot,*" ungrammatical as it was, appealed to her: it made the noun collective, as if all human beings were possessed of a common, built-in flaw that made them prone to stumble and fall. *Their foot shall slide in due time:* it was fore-ordained, imperially decreed: in a word, *designed.*

She wondered what in her upbringing made this idea so appealing to her. There had been no religion at all in her childhood; her mother had started going to church only after her father died. If anything in her life explained it, she thought, shifting the seatbelt which was cutting into her breast, it would have to be her father's alcoholism. It had made her see the world as arbitrary, unpredictable. When her father was sober, their lives were normal, even dull; when he was drunk, their world was turned upside down. Lightning bolts of rage could erupt out of the blue, her mother could be transformed from an intelligent woman into a cringing creature wringing her hands in the corner. Since there was nothing Elizabeth could do as a child to effect any change in her father's behavior (though she had spent years trying), she had given up the project and become fatalistic. If life was a matter of fate, nothing was your fault, which was a comfort of sorts.

Her father wasn't a bad man, only a bewildering one, trying many times to quit drinking but never succeeding. He had died of cirrhosis of the liver eight years ago; not the worst way to go, in Elizabeth's opinion. He was in hospital for several weeks, his consciousness dimming and gradually fading out until at the end he slipped into a coma. The whole process had seemed worse for the rest of the family than for him, particularly for her mother, who had sat beside him hour after hour in those last days. His body had given off a terrible smell, which he himself was blissfully unaware of, unless, Elizabeth thought, being in a coma was some particularly awful kind of hell where you still registered sensation but couldn't communicate with anyone. Like in the paralysis nightmares she used to have years ago, where she would find herself in a darkened room reaching to turn on the light, but the bulb would fade and burn out, leaving her helpless in the darkness, unable to move, struggling desperately to wriggle just one finger…

The nightmares had always terrified her. She shuddered, remembering, and cut the memory short, forcing herself to concentrate on the white line running down the center of the road. The ball game droned on.

*   *   *   *

When they arrived home, Stephen and Philip escaped to their friend Andy's, whose house had a backyard pool. Walter unpacked the hamper and put two beers in the freezer. Then he turned on the air conditioning and the living room television set, intent on pursuing the game.

"Shall we eat around six?" Elizabeth asked. "I was thinking just an omelet, which can be made any time."

"Six is fine," he said without looking up, "or whenever the boys get back."

"I'll be upstairs reading then," she said.

The game, in its middle innings, would last at least another hour. She went up to her sewing room and closed the door. Then she opened Henry's diary and began to read.

January 4

The Clod and the Pebble

"Love seeketh not itself to please
Nor for itself hath any care
But for another gives its ease
And builds a Heaven in Hell's despair."

So sang a little clod of clay
Trodden with the cattle's feet

But a pebble of the brook
Warbled out these meters mete:

"Love seeketh only self to please
To bind another to its delight
Joys in another's loss of ease
And builds a Hell in Heaven's despite.

I was reading Blake's poems again the other night, which I first discovered in the prison library at Allenwood. I'm considering using this one in next month's leaflet. Or perhaps the poem that appeared in the last issue of *Fellowship* by a man named Stanton Coblentz:

Never before, since cavemen's clubs and brands,
Such towers of defense in many lands!
And never have great nations felt so tense
Crushed by the master foe, their own defense.

This is less "literary" than Blake's, and if I want to gain the respect of these researchers, all of whom hold PhD's, Blake would probably be a better choice than Coblentz. I assume they would recognize the name.

Blake's poem is a dialogue, and a dialogue is what I want to create—among the researchers themselves, if not with me. What strikes me about it is that Blake never says who has the better of the debate. The humble clod is singing his peace/love/harmony message while being trodden under the cattle's feet. But surely that is preferable to building a hell in heaven's despite?

I hope at least to introduce them to the idea that the "clod" has a point of view. I keep seeing the poem in terms of a dialogue between militarism and non-violence. I'll try it in the next leaflet, and maybe use the Coblentz as a take-off point for the one after that.

Elizabeth raised her eyes from the page. Despite the fan and the open window, it felt as if the heat of the entire afternoon had collected in this room. She crossed to the window and opened it wider. There would be more air circulation if she opened the door, but she felt safer with it closed. That was absurd, of course, a closed door in such weather was more likely to arouse suspicion and invite questions than an open one. She compromised, opening it part-way and securing it with a chunk of jadeite from the clutter on her desk. Then she selected a book from the bookshelf and placed it in the chair beside her. If she heard Walter on the stairs, she would pretend to be reading it. It was like that old trick from school, hiding what you really wanted to read under the official reader.

Through the window she could hear the tangled chirping of birds and the sound of the man across the street mowing his lawn. It was a peaceful sound, but the man must be seriously bored to be mowing his lawn at this time of the day. It wasn't good for the grass.

She wondered what it had been like for Henry in prison. She couldn't remember how long his sentence had been; Walter must have told her at the time but she couldn't recall. Less than a year, she imagined, his "crime" hadn't been serious: trespassing on government property, or something like that. But how long even a few weeks in prison must seem! She couldn't imagine it. At least, she thought, he had access to a library. He seemed to have made good use of it.

She went back to the Blake poem and read it again. It disturbed her that she couldn't say for sure whose "side" Blake was on; or which side she herself favored, for that matter. Wasn't the clod an idiot to be "warbling out meters sweet" while getting himself trampled? On the other hand, pebbles wounded, they bruised the heel. The stony-hearted selfishness Blake attributes to them was the source of all kinds of grief.

Though maybe you weren't supposed to choose, she thought, maybe Blake was just stating that that's the way things were, that some people were clods and some were pebbles. The pebbles were more numerous, and probably had greater survival value; that, however, didn't make them right.

She gave it up and went on to the next entry.

January 5

Sometimes I find myself homesick for the family. Mother isn't well and keeps asking to see me. I told her I would take the bus down next weekend; she thanked me and assured me Walter wouldn't be there. And Jenine? I asked. "No," she said, "why should she be? She's busy with her work, like everyone else." Too bad: Jenine is the only member of the family who makes me feel accepted, the only one who doesn't seem to want to pick a quarrel.

I used to feel that way about Sylvie when we were kids. She was always so kind. She was just nineteen when she died; Jenine was only a year old, and I barely fourteen. Funny to think that Jenine is older now than Sylvie lived to be. I confess she's the loveliest novice nun I've ever seen. I still think of her as my "baby sister" rather than as my niece. She is what Sylvie might have become had she been allowed to live.

I don't think Mom has ever recovered from Sylvie's death, even now; her name is rarely mentioned. Sylvie's lover never knew she was pregnant; he died in Vietnam before she could tell him, one of those unlucky enough to be killed while on his very first patrol. I never knew him, though I wish I had. Sylvie hadn't known him long either, I don't think they went out on more than three or four dates between the time he left basic training and the time he was shipped out, but he must have been a good man or she wouldn't have loved him.

Mom adored Jenine, and wasn't the least bit bothered that she hadn't come in a package with a marriage license. Both she and Sylvie were proud of her. She would be even prouder if she knew her now.

January 6

The lack of response to my leaflets, together with the dreary weather, is taking a toll. I am beginning to detest the politeness in my voice, when I don't feel in the least polite. It's seems to me more urgent all the time for the world to wake up, before it's too late. I should probably stop listening to the news each night, which has become my dinner ritual. The planet seems to be in extraordinary turmoil. Are these adjustments to the new shifts Gorbachev is making in the Soviet Union?

The number of terrorist incidents is increasing, the discotheque bombing in Germany a few weeks ago one of a string. The CIA claims the new villain behind it all is Khadafy. It's hard to believe that he cold be so stupid: too many stings can drive an elephant mad. Why on earth do terrorists think that terror accomplishes anything?

January 9

The imbecilic war-posturing of Khadafy and Reagan continues, with the press egging Reagan on to "put up to shut up." He has instituted unilateral economic sanctions against Libya (Europe is refusing to participate), frozen Libyan assets, ordered all 1500 Americans working there to come home or face jail, which some claim is unconstitutional. This morning's paper carried a picture of a California used-car lot owner standing beside a sign that said "Honk if you want Khadafy trashed." A Maine radio station is advising people to wrap their garbage in packages and send it to him. Khadafy, meanwhile, is in his element, boasting and swaggering like an inebriated rooster.

At first I thought all this was harmless; but now I wonder whether it's a collision of psychoses. For the first time Khadafy interjected the Crusades into his name-calling, saying that Americans were, among other things, "stinking Crusaders." He is an outrageous clown, a buffoon like Idi Amin (though not as murderous). Amin never tweaked the eagle's feathers like this. No one has, not even Castro in his heyday.

Is this shadow-boxing or a farcical prelude to Armageddon? The world could be annihilated in just such a way. What if Russia steps in and lays down some line and tells the US not to cross it?

January 14

Spent the weekend at Abbottsford, mostly shoveling snow. Mom is going in for a hysterectomy on the first of March. Fibroids, nothing cancerous, but the doctors think it better to remove it. She'll be at Grace Hospital in Baltimore. Insists she doesn't need for me to be there, that Walter and Elizabeth will come, and father, of course. I always interpret this to mean she doesn't want her two sons in the same room together. When I asked her this directly, she said, "Not when I'm in a hospital bed," admitting she was afraid of the stress.

So because Walter doesn't want to see me, I'm shut out of the hospital. This seems unjust.

OK, it's unjust: get used to it. It's what she wants that counts.

Jan 16

Gorbachev has made an extraordinary offer of a phased plan to eliminate, by the year 2000, all nuclear weapons. Even more extraordinary, Reagan is only half-calling it propaganda. I'm beginning to think he actually does want to get rid of such weapons but is a prisoner of his Cabinet. I can hear the advisers now: "Nuclear nakedness? Unthinkable." They will translate the text of the proposal and present it to him in the most negative light. Edward Teller will be called in to tell him what a bad idea a nuclear-free world would be, how without our missiles we will be impotent. Treasury will be called in too to report the consequences to the economy if the nuclear arms race should end......On the other hand, they can't keep dismissing these Russian offers as propaganda. Gorbachev has called their hand.

I am daring to hope.

Talked to mom, as I promised I would. The doctor has given her something to help her sleep. She sounded almost cheerful.

Elizabeth glanced at her watch. It was time to call the boys and remind them to come home, time to see how many eggs there were in the refrigerator and what was on hand to make a salad with, after which she wanted to take a shower and wash her hair. She didn't want to read any more about nuclear weapons and foreign affairs, or anything that reminded her of how dangerous and stupid the world was.

It was intriguing to see how Henry's mind worked though, to experience, in some part, what it felt like to be inside his skin. She liked it. She would read more later, even if it was disturbing. It would be like the secret treasures she used to keep as a child, her collection of stones wrapped in a handkerchief and buried beneath the forsythia bush, that she could take out and play with whenever she wanted. She was grateful he had given it to her.

She concealed it in her bottom desk drawer under a pile of old bills. Then she went downstairs to call the boys.

CHAPTER 6

▼

When Souls are outlawed, Hearts are sick
Hearts being sick, Mind nothing can....

From a poem by e. e. cummings: another poet I discovered in the prison library. Can't remember the rest of it. Maybe I should have taken literature courses in college instead of wasting two years at Peabody playing the piano. Two years to realize I didn't have the talent I thought I had. And then there was Vietnam and the protest movement, and reading Gandhi and joining the commune. I had no money to go back to school even if I'd wanted to, which I didn't.

1970: my first pacifist action, my first visit to Edgewood Arsenal. Walking with eighty others for five days, ten miles each day, taking turns carrying our seedling pines, behind us banners saying SERVE HUMAN NEEDS, RESEARCH FOR LIFE, NOT DEATH. On our way from Washington to plant a pine tree, first at Fort Detrick, where the weapons were tested, then on to Edgewood, where they are designed. The pine tree, as we explained in our leaflet, was the logo on the original American Revolutionary flag, a symbol of the Tree of Life.

The Fort Detrick people let us in, even helped with the planting, aware that without conflict there would be no story for the journalists, and with no story, no publicity. The folks at Edgewood weren't as smart. We were refused entry, and had to spend the night sleeping beside the road, waiting till the next morning when the gates had to be opened to let the workers through. When that happened, we planned to commit civil disobedience by walking through the gates, two at a time, one person carrying the seedling tree, the other a yellow watering can and a small plastic spade with a bright red handle that couldn't possibly be mistaken for a weapon.

Once the workers' cars had passed through, two of our group, an elderly man named Gordon Schiffman and his wife Elise, walked slowly forward, carrying the seedling pine. As they approached, the guards closed and padlocked the gates. An official read the riot act over a bullhorn, ordering them to leave. The Schiffmans remained where they were, asking courteous questions of the guards, who wouldn't answer.

Since we had been careful to notify the press of our intentions to break the law, several reporters were there. The spectacle wasn't looking good for the government. Finally, when the gates were open to let the workers go home, the Schiffmans managed to step across onto "government property." The minute they did, an armored car with M.P.'s in it materialized from around a bend in the road, for all in the world as if there was a bomb in our flower pot, not a seedling pine. The pot, interestingly, was never searched, but its bearers were marched into the armored car. Since government workers in cars were still leaving, they were unable to close the gates. Two more of us therefore went through to pick up the tree, which was lying on its side, half-spilled out of its container. We walked calmly, slowly, careful to do nothing provocative. The onlookers, including the press, watched in silence, as again the armored car roared around the bend the minute we moved three steps beyond the gates.

It went on like this for over an hour; seventy people were arrested, two by two. It was my first detention. We were released twelve hours later, the sentence suspended. The government didn't want more publicity, certainly not the kind they were getting. Even ordinary reporters reacted to the sight of an armored car bearing down on a seedling pine and wrote sympathetic articles. A baby tree of life versus a massive military machine: David vs. Goliath, Bambi vs. Godzilla.

In reality it was more a confrontation between two types of people, a piece of street theater dramatizing two opposing philosophies: planting trees versus killing trees. We clapped and sang, they scowled. Right was on our side.

The government didn't see it that way, of course; nor did my brother. He was only in his first year of graduate school, but even then he was very conservative politically. The day after the protest, we met for a walk in the park. I thought it was for a friendly good-bye, since I was leaving to go back to the commune the next day. But the encounter turned into something vicious, an extraordinary argument over non-violence that ended with Walter "proving his point" by suddenly shoving me and knocking me to the ground. In response I lay there unresisting (proving *my* point, I suppose), moving only to cover my head with my arms. He proceeded to kick me hard, in the ribs, then picked up a handful of dirt (I could see him sideways through my arms), and threw it at me contemptuously before turning and walking away.

I picked myself up and went back to Kentucky. My Old Kentucky Commune: my substitute family.

I was right to have left, I think, but right also to have come back here. I wrestled too long with the question of whether my motives were impure, whether I was partly struggling to defeat my brother rather than bearing witness against chemical weapons. The question also preoccupied me at Allenwood, after my second arrest, as well as at the commune. I finally concluded that motives for any action are always hopelessly entangled and that waiting for absolute clarity was an excuse for sloth. I decided to go where my conscience pulled me.

Sometimes I think that I am doing this for Martin Halladay, who I heard speak back at Jonah House in Baltimore early in the seventies. I'd gone to see Peter Watkins' film, *The War Game*, I remember, a film on nuclear war made for the BBC but banned by the British government, and also from American theaters, shown only in university film clubs and church basements. Naturally I was curious to know why. After I saw it, I understood: I doubt if anyone who sees this film ever forgets it, or ever again think abstractly about nuclear war. It is horror made flesh; hell no longer a metaphor.

Halladay is in prison now for the most recent Ploughshares action. Sentenced to eight years for taking a hammer and spray-painting with his blood the word NO on the concrete lid of a nuclear missile silo in Missouri. He sang hymns while awaiting his arrest. What he said at his trial, quoted in the Ploughshares newsletter, was that though each of us isn't called to take a hammer to a missile silo, "each of us is called to act as if the future of this planet matters."

That's why I stand outside the gates of Edgewood Arsenal, "futile" as it may be: trying to act as if the future of this planet matters.

Elizabeth put the notebook down. It was almost two in the morning; everyone else was asleep. She sat in her rocking chair in the sewing room, reading by the light of one small lamp. She knew she should be thinking of ways to help the future, but all she could think about was Henry: his loneliness seemed to jump off the page at her, no matter what he was writing about. This was the longest entry in the book; she wondered at the time he must have on his hands to be able to write at such length.

It was touching, what he had written, but rather shocking. Walter had never mentioned Henry's original protest at Edgewood, which must have happened before she and Walter had met. Was Henry's opposition to weapons engineering yet another reason for Walter having argued so strongly to take the job at the lab? He had told her he and Henry had quarreled once over pacifism, but not in any detail, nor that a specific protest demonstration of Henry's had triggered the argument. She certainly would have remembered had she been told that he had kicked his brother and thrown dirt at him: the picture it conjured up was chilling.

A streak of lightning lit up the sky beyond the window. The curtains stirred. It would rain, she thought, thank god; it had been unbearably close all day. She stood up and leaned against the window. Another jagged lightning bolt lit up great puffy masses of cloud, sending a shiver of anticipation down her spine. Let it explode, she thought, let it crash and bang and discharge all that tension. Let it rain, let it rain.

A cool breeze bathed her face as the first few drops began to fall. They gathered in strength, and became a steady drumbeat. She stayed at the window for a long time, listening. Then she closed it and put the diary away.

The next morning she was tired and irritable, and found it a relief when Walter left for work. She dropped the boys at the park to watch a Little League game, with money for treats and the bus home, then shopped at the Piggly-Wiggly for groceries. Annoyingly, a man in front of her was holding up the line asking about prices and deciding he didn't really need certain items after all. Once home, she put the groceries away and fixed herself a glass of iced tea, which she carried to the living room, together with a bag of pretzel sticks. She was determined to finish the diary, in one uninterrupted sitting.

January 28

I woke up to the news that the Challenger had exploded this morning, killing all seven astronauts aboard. *Mission Control, There has been a Major Malfunction.* Seven dead; and twelve billion up in smoke. How many people could be fed with that, how many wells dug? Seven astronauts die and we have a national cry-in. It is sad, as any unexpected and undeserved death is, but meanwhile seventy kids starved to death in Haiti, seventeen were tortured in Chile, 70,000 died of preventable disease, seventy more street kids killed by police in Brazil.

Man-in-the-street interviews in various parts of the country suggest the average American believes it was Russian or Libyan sabotage that caused the shuttle to explode. What lies beneath this willful denial that accidents can happen, even to the best-designed machine? People have a frightening faith in technology: the assumption that our nuclear reactors will never fail, that our bombs will never go off, could lead to collective doom. I suppose this kind of denial is protective; the reality, for some, may be too crazy, too frightening to live with. But it seems a mal-adaptive response.

February 4

While I was in Baltimore last week, I went to a showing of the Polish film, *Man of Iron,* about Lech Walesa and the Solidarity movement. North Americans are so alienated and isolated from each other they seem incapable of even imagining collective action. I sense among American writers something bordering on envy for their Eastern counterparts, like Poland, where a sense of community and "solidarity" exists, or did during the eighties.

The miracle of Solidarity was that people overcame their sense of powerlessness and came together, united by a common oppression, a common Church, and brave men like Michnik and Walesa. The film is a study in non-violent revolution, of people "acting in the present as they would wish the state to be acting in the future"—that is, acting according to conscience.

Non-violent protest is a way of shaming the Powers-That-Be into changing. If one reason they cling to power is the fear of what would happen if they lost it, non-violence can lessen that fear. It partially disarms them, leaving them with only a threadbare ideology that they themselves no longer believe in. The film seems to suggest that a non-violent revolution is more an evolution, a process of changing man's habits of thinking. When a critical number of people is reached, action may emerge spontaneously, and bring about political change.

February 17

I came down with some bug or other last Friday, hopefully not one of the super-ones they used to breed at Detrick. All weekend I could barely get out of bed. Vigilled during the week, though it was difficult. The chest pains are gone now and the cough has almost subsided, but I'm still too tired at night to do anything, not even read.

Mrs. J's check for the dry walling I did last month hasn't come yet and the rent is due. My rice stock is getting low, though I still have a month's worth of potatoes from the garden. I should plant more vegetables this spring, though I remember thinking last September I'd never be able to eat my way through this year's crop. More corn next time, and limas. More kale.

February 28

Unbelievably, there have been two—count 'em, *two* non-violent "revolutions" within the last week—the Haitian people suddenly coming alive and shrugging off the tyranny of "Baby Doc" Duvalier, and the people of the Philippines ridding themselves of the Marcos regime. Two astonishing examples of people suddenly coming together (as in the Polish film about Solidarity) and saying, "Look, the Emperor has no clothes," whereupon the Emperor is revealed as naked as a plucked chicken, and runs away.

To hear our press tell it, both revolutions are owing, at least in part, to our Fearless Leader Reagan, who was magnanimity itself in allowing Marcos (a "close friend," after all) to fall. (Reagan has offered him sanctuary in Hawaii, incidentally; I think Duvalier is going to France). Still, whatever the press spin, People Power has proved it can work. The mystery is, why now and not before? Both Marcos and the two Duvaliers have been standing on their peoples' necks and robbing them blind for decades.

With any luck it will be the joyous images of the crowds dancing in the streets of Manila that will prove contagious.

March 5

I spent the weekend in Baltimore, in order to be close at hand if anything went wrong with mom's operation. Talked to her on the phone before the procedure and again when she was in the recovery room. Both times she thanked me, tearfully, for doing as she asked and not coming to the hospital. Walter and Elizabeth were there, and my father, of course. Apparently she is recovering well and there are no complications. My father must be relieved. So am I.

The doctors predict a full recovery, i.e., regaining her old energy, though this may take up to six months and she should get plenty of rest. We must talk about hiring a cleaning lady, though she is likely to resist the idea. I'm sure she'll feel robbed of her place if her housekeeping is taken away; it's part of the rhythm of her day, and I gather that at that age you don't like to have your patterns interrupted. It may make the difference between feeling useful and feeling useless.

It was lonely in Baltimore. I stayed at Mark's, who was cordial but somehow removed. Problems of his own, I imagine; he still hasn't recovered from Donna's leaving him, though that happened almost two years ago. My melancholy persisted in the train on the way back, where out the window it was raining, with few signs of spring.

I am making little progress in the leafleting. Almost no one is accepting them now. I sometimes think I'd reach more people if I had them plasticized and tossed them in Chesapeake Bay.

March 17

While fixing dinner tonight I turned on the news, mostly for the company, and got more than I bargained for. Reagan seems to have lost his mind in his attempt to get Congress to cough up a hundred million dollars in aid for the Contras. He has gone on television claiming that Nicaragua is a Soviet base, that it's full of Iranians and Libyans and who knows, maybe the Red Brigades. The amount of vituperation pouring out through the media is like nothing I've ever heard.

A sample of the Great Communicator's intelligence and wit: in answer to a reporter's comment that Ortega had said he'd lost his senses over Nicaragua, Reagan replied belligerently, "Takes one to know one." Nyah, nyah. Are these people adults?

March 22

We have set off another huge underground nuclear explosion, the government's implicit answer to Gorbachev's proposed moratorium on testing. The media continue to spew out garbage on Nicaragua, interviewing Contras over and over, never interviewing any supporters of the Sandinistas. The latter have been ruled out of bounds: they are officially the "enemy," and interviewing the enemy could be construed as "treason." The fear of being seen as disloyal or "leftist" makes most reporters bend over backwards to prove how true blue they are.

So the misinformation machine is running at full speed. Where is *our* Fairness in Media group?

March 23

My father bought himself a new camera and camera bag recently, which he showed me the last time I was there. The bag is made of a new material that is apparently indestructible. I much admired it, but it raised a question, namely, whether we can have all this amazing technology without the poisons created in the process of producing it. Can our technologies ever be toilet-trained, so to speak, or are they inherently, cumulatively, murderous? Even if their manufacture didn't release toxins into the air and water, simply disposing of all their "indestructible" corpses when they wear out or go out of fashion is a serious problem. At some point we'll need the whole of the earth just to cover our discards.

Nothing should be allowed to be manufactured that is not biodegradable. Either that or we had better start genetically engineering bacteria especially designed to degrade it.

Scientific believers like my brother think that whatever problems are created by new technologies can be solved by still newer technologies, such as DNA splicing. Each new "discovery" gives fresh impetus (afflatus?) to the myth of progress. It is only later that we see the price tag and realize that the fix really didn't really solve the problem, that more often than not it has created a host of bigger ones— cf. plutonium, nerve gas, DDT, Agent Orange.

I didn't say anything remotely like this to my father, of course, just expressed the hope that he would enjoy his new purchase. Maybe photographing things will get him to go outside in the fields and move around more, which would be good. He is getting too heavy.

March 24

The US has attacked Libya, claiming a Libyan ship fired on one of our planes. Shades of the Gulf of Tonkin. In retaliation, we have bombed a missile base and sank the ship in question. No word of casualties. Now what?

March 25

The networks reported last night that two battalion of Nicaraguan troops had invaded Honduras and that the Honduran government had requested twenty million dollars in emergency military aid from the U.S. I was astonished: what an utterly stupid thing for the Sandinistas to have done, I thought, what extraordinarily bad timing. Turns out it's not true: the story this evening is that the Honduran government has denied there was any such invasion, or that it had ever requested any aid. By 11:00, on *Nightline*, the "invasion" had been demoted to an "incursion." CBS reported Hondurans as saying that the original story was an "exaggeration," part of Reagan's "propaganda build-up." On PBS the Nicaraguan Ambassador categorically denied that there were any Nicaraguan troops in Honduras, or ever had been.

One of these governments is lying. If it is the U.S., did they dress up some Contras in Sandinista uniforms and send them to "invade Honduras" (as Hitler dressed up German troops in Polish uniforms in order to claim that Poland had invaded Germany)? Whatever the case, Reagan will get away with it, for who can believe a U.S. president would tell a barefaced lie? Communists are by definition liars; the Sandinistas are Communists; ergo Ronnie must be telling the truth.

Alice in Wonderland logic.

March 27

I dreamed last night of discovering a young girl lying in a meadow with a straw hat concealing her face. The whole scene was vaguely like a Renoir painting; she was wearing a long white dress with a blue ribbon threaded through the hem. I approached her, thinking she was asleep, and stood there admiring the picture she made. Then she turned her head and revealed her face, and I saw it was Jenine. She smiled at me, not in invitation but as a gesture of sympathy and comfort. "Sylvie?" I said, though I knew it was Jenine and that Sylvie was dead. But it was as if Sylvie was using Jenine as her medium to communicate with me.

If so, she succeeded. I woke up this morning with the memory of her smile and felt my spirits lift. I had stayed up late watching *Night Line*, which was devoted to Libya and the new "electronic warfare" this country is waging. For the first time the Navy is using its new generation of high-tech computerized weapons: it is their first test on an actual battlefield.

The program was curiously obscene, like a romance of high-tech death. Its point was that America now has a foolproof electronic shield against which the most modern Russian-made missiles (the SAM-5's that Libya was using) are powerless. Electronic scrambling devices totally confuse the guidance systems of any incoming missile, making it veer off its mark. Meanwhile, our own missiles hone in with perfect accuracy and successfully destroy the enemy's radar and take out whatever targets they please. The "surgical strike" has been perfected.

Was this Libyan action a smoke screen to cover the Big Lie Reagan got away with on Nicaragua? The Contra issue is off the news: four minutes of *Nightline* were devoted to an update, namely that Congress has authorized the $20,000,000 Reagan asked for. The Nicaraguan troops, "badly mauled" by the Contras, are said to be retreating in disarray back across the border. If, of course, they ever crossed the border in the first place.

March 29

The violets are out, the maples putting out their delicate gold-red beginnings. Fresh grass needling up, the tulips sporting pale green, unopened buds. The world giddy with spring.

Dreamed of Jenine again. This time it was definitely Jenine.

Her attention was broken by the ringing of the telephone. She made no move to answer it: whoever it was would just have to call back. On the eighth ring it stopped, but by then she had already gone to the bathroom and discovered that her period had come, which puzzled her because, unless she was mistaken, it was unusually early. She counted back; the last one had come the night of the Winslows' party, two Fridays ago, which made this one a full week early. She was usually quite regular; surely she wasn't becoming peri-menopausal at thirty-six? She stared at the reddish brown stain on the toilet tissue, then shrugged. Better early than late, she thought, better than discovering that her IUD wasn't working and she was pregnant. Lovely as her boys were, the last thing she wanted right now was another child.

She extracted a tampon from the dainty pink and white box she kept in the cabinet under the sink, its baby-powder scent wafting through the air when released from its pink plastic holder. How pure and white it was when it went in, and fresh-smelling, to help you forget the stink a few hours later when you pulled it out. She deposited the holder in the wastebasket, and returned to the sofa.

March 31

Predictably, no one is calling Reagan on his lie: officially, the "Sandinista invasion" of Honduras is now a "minor incursion." Reagan "exaggerated," the pundits chorus, you know how he is; it was a white lie, not a black one. The U.S. is also now admitting that the bombing exercise in Libya was planned three months ago, as punishment for "terrorist acts." We are again assured that Untruth in the name of a Good Cause is perfectly OK. Great Powers are expected to lie, aren't they? Cf. Machiavelli. Cf. Henry Kissinger.

April 10

There was another underground nuclear test today; one hundred resisters were arrested at the test site in Nevada. Also the House passed a law *loosening* gun control. It is now easier to get a gun in the U.S. than a library card. Sixty people a day are killed with hand guns.

April 15

Last night, at 7:00 our time (2:00 a.m. in Tripoli), the U.S. bombed five "terrorist targets" in a "retaliatory self-defense strike"—a choice Orwellian phrase, so nicely antiseptic. The "terrorist targets" included Khadafy's palace and his sixteen-month-old adopted daughter, who was killed. Two of his sons, ages five and four, were wounded, together with his wife. Khadafy himself has not appeared or been heard from; he may be dead. He was the target, of course: the family members were "collateral damage."

If all this is true, one can only say Wow, behold, everyone: the U.S. now has precision technology that can kill you in your own palace, even in your personal bunker. I should think the rest of the world would be so impressed they'd immediately sign a surrender treaty; or alternatively, move to a boycott of all things American. How about a worldwide petition pledging that until the U.S. renounces its policy of unilaterally attacking foreign countries and agrees to a multilateral reduction of nuclear arms, we the peoples of the world will refrain from buying American products?

Am I the only one frightened by the concentration of so much power in the hands of one nation, the leader of which apparently believes in astrology, in addition to being seriously senile?

April 30

Two days ago, but only reported yesterday, there was a major accident at the Chernobyl nuclear reactor, near Kiev. As many as two thousand people may have been killed. The Dnieper River has been contaminated. The reactor is still on fire, with apparently no way of putting the fire out.

Sweden and Finland are reporting ten times background radiation levels; the cloud also passed into Poland, but is apparently now blowing back across Russia. One expert on NBC added that there is a 50/50 chance of a major reactor accident in the U.S. within the next decade.

All day long I've been hearing Donne's refrain, "Never send to know for whom the bell tolls, it tolls for thee."

The earth seems to be lurching again. "Lurches" are the times in history when the web of life is shaken so severely we all feel the tremors. Something that makes us collectively feel our common mortality, forces us to look at our common fate.

Kiev, Kiev, ancient beautiful city, have they made you uninhabitable? Poisoned the land, the water, the people? It is not forgivable. Will a tragedy of this enormity wake anyone up—the French, for example? They are the most heavily dependent in Europe on nuclear power.

If the Russians do not provide full disclosure about this, it will be another of their crimes against humanity.

May 1

Now it's a game of "who do you believe?" The Soviets are denying "thousands dead," showing pictures of the reactor, with no fire. They claim 197 were hospitalized for radiation illness. Ham radios have picked up different messages, however, which corroborate the American version. In Poland, 500 kilometers away, some food has already been irradiated. Children are being given doses of iodine.

The big question is whether the world will see this as an "act of God," or see it as man-made and rebel against it. It is clearly a warning, but only if we draw the right conclusions. The Europeans, I gather, are furious, but at the Russians, not at nuclear technology.

May 5

Chernobyl has been eased off the news, though the fallout is now polluting Austria. It's also in the upper atmosphere over the mid-west, coming soon to a neighborhood near you.

Headline today, re the G-7 meeting: *Rockets and Radioactive Rain Hit Tokyo Summit.* Maggie Thatcher, unfazed by the prospect, was quoted as saying to Nakasone, "Let's go outside to show we aren't afraid." Nakasone demurred, answering "Safety first."

They put out a mild statement condemning the Russians for their secrecy. I gather it's unseemly to say anything too harsh about your enemy's nuclear reactors when you have them too.

May 8

The Chernobyl reactor is still burning, almost two weeks after the accident started, smoldering like a two-ton chunk of charcoal, threatening to melt the cement floor and make contact with the underground water table, which could cause a Hiroshima-type explosion. I feel such pity for the people who live there, so many of whom will die prematurely, even if there is no explosion. Some western scientists are predicting up to 10,000 cases of cancer, and increased rates of leukemia.

ABC ran a story tonight saying that the Hanford nuclear plant in Washington state released *one million radioactive curies* in the late 40's, partly on an "experimental" basis to test the government's monitoring equipment. This information was deliberately withheld "in order to protect U.S. nuclear weapons, which were then in their infancy." The authorities deny any health effects, but the camera traveled with a victim down what he called "the mile of death," where every house along the way had people in them who have died or are dying of cancer. Exposure to radiation not only can cause cancer, it accelerates the growth of already existing tumors.

What if Dan Rather and Tom Brokaw had delivered the news of the disaster at Chernobyl with the emotion it deserves, what if they had let tears come to their eyes? Would it be contagious? Surely it would put a dent in our habitual denial. We bottle up our pity and our fear, shut them out, deny their validity.

Dan Rather would probably be fired if he cried. Is this because they are afraid we might reconnect our heads and our hearts? For woe be to the Nuclear Age if that ever happens.

I connect most peoples' acceptance of the Bomb with some deep denial of their connection to and dependence on Mother Earth. Our most dangerous fantasy is that we can transcend nature by flying off into the sky, somehow living above it. But "Nature" is not just the landscape: it is the air we breathe, the water we drink, the food we consume. All of them are being poisoned: by plutonium, sulfur dioxide, plastic…. And the fantasy of flying away and taking up residence on the moon is puerile. Even if were possible, we'd just reconstruct there the mess we've already made down here.

This society seems unmoored, as if we have lost touch with what is solid and are drifting off into an unreal stratosphere. We know how to destroy the earth, but not how to take care of it.

The only sense I can make of the concept of Original Sin is to see it as our fatal ability to abstract ourselves from our senses, to literally take leave of them. As if the problem is how to escape the earth, or blow it up, rather than how to live on it.

May 14

They have released the startling information that the present level of radiation is now comparable to what it was during the fifties, when we were still doing atmospheric testing. The main concern is Iodine-21 and Strontium-90. They are testing milk daily all over the country. Still, they tell us we are not to get "hysterical," that this level of radiation is "harmless." This is another contradiction, for if it's all so safe, why did we ban atmospheric testing in 1963?

May 28

I was considering doing an essay for this month's pamphlet called "Calling Things By Their Right Names," but then I questioned my own presumption. Is God's name God or Yahweh or Allah?

In the beginning was the Silence. But later three men claimed to hear the voice of God, and each wrote down what he heard. Each proclaimed the words he had heard were sacred, every last one of them, and commanded his followers to persecute and shun anyone who denied the sacredness of the least of these words. The men who heard the voices were the followers of Moses and Mohammed and

Christ: the People of the Book, the Iroquois called them. They didn't know about the Vedas and the Hindu's, or they might well have included them too.

There can be no fundamentalist tyranny if you lack a sacred text. I'm with the Quakers: we should stick with Silence.

June 1

An odd "breakthrough" this morning: one of the men driving through the gates rolled down his window and accepted a pamphlet, at the same time slipping me a note. He made no eye contact, and quickly drove off. The note asked to meet me at the Blue Dolphin restaurant in Chestertown next Saturday at two. Chestertown is thirty miles from here; I'll have to see when the buses run.

I hope this person is genuine and not a security man in disguise. Either way, I'm happy to talk to him.

June 5

Working steadily at painting jobs when I'm not standing outside at the gates. Also watering and tending the garden; there has been little rain. Curious to meet my mystery man tomorrow. There is a bus that leaves in the morning and departs at four. I will have a two/three hour wait; but I've never been to Chestertown, and it must have some attractions.

June 7

Met X, who doesn't want me repeating his name. Over beer and crab cakes we talked. For the most part this involved my answering his questions about my motives, what I hoped to achieve, the usual. We argued some about my Big-Eye pamphlet. He stood his ground, but not, it seemed to me, with complete conviction. He said he was speaking to me out of curiosity; he knows that Walter and I are brothers and wondered if my daily vigils were partly a matter of sibling rivalry. I tried to explain as best I could.

He is a likable man; also, I suspect, a morally troubled one. He seems very uptight about his job, which makes it hard to believe that he met with me out of mere curiosity. It is possible, of course, that my credulity is being played upon and he's gathering information for Security, but if so, he's welcome. Everything I am doing is well within the guarantees of the U.S. Constitution; I have nothing to hide that violates any laws—no pot plants, no under-the-table money, not even any traffic tickets (one of the benefits of not owning a car).

X doesn't seem to understand that the Constitution protects his right to meet with me, to think thoughts his bosses don't want him to think, even to speak them in public if he chooses. It might mean losing his job, of course: the right to both speak your mind AND keep your government job is not, alas, Constitutionally guaranteed. So it did take courage for him to meet with me.

I think it went well; he suggested meeting again, though at some unspecified time.

At least now I will have an audience in my mind when I write future pamphlets, something flesh and blood, with features different from my brother's.

In the four hours I had to wait before our meeting, I took a pleasant stroll around Washington College, founded by Kent County shortly after the Revolutionary War, with the fifty guinea reward the county received for supplying the troops with flour. A pleasant campus, with benches and a nice view of the Bay. Had lunch in the cafeteria.

June 20

A report on the news that a quarter million sheep and lambs in Cumbria and Wales have been found to have excessive radiation levels and will be kept off the market. There was Chernobyl cesium in the grass the poor creatures were eating. I couldn't get this out of my head, and when I came home, looked up Blake's poem in my anthology. I re-read it, and wrote the following:

> Little radioactive lamb, who made thee?
> Dost thou know who made thee?
> Gave thee life and bade thee feed
> On the cesium-encrusted mead?

> He is called Modern Man
> Maker of monsters he refuses to ban
> Chooses death and calls it power
> Mutely waits his final hour.

> Little victim lamb, God bless thee.
> Little victim lamb, God bless thee.

June 22

Hooray for Gorbachev, who has abolished Glavlit, throwing some 80,000 censors out of work. What a contrast with over here, where the Democrats just passed another $100,000,000 authorization for the murderous Contras.

I started Breyten Breytenbach's *Confessions of an Albino Terrorist* this evening. The second paragraph asks the age-old Buddhist questions, "What did your face look like before you were born? What did you look like before your parents were born? Where were you then? In fact, where do you come from?" Having just finished Primo Levi's *The Periodic Tables*, I found myself replying, "I come from something that happened on the molecular level, some combining of Carbon with Oxygen and Phosphorus. And when I die, the carbon atoms will rearrange themselves and carry on elsewhere." For some reason, this was a comforting thought.

July 1

The US now admits to having fifty operational Stealth bombers. An obscene word, *stealth*: coming like a thief in the night, carrying Megadeath. Fifty of them: sleek mechanical pterodactyls, carrion birds of prey.

I'll be spending the 4th of July weekend at Abbottsford. Walter will be there; but so will Jenine.

July 4

A pleasant bus ride this morning; sat next to a jovial black woman who wanted to know what I did for a living. I said I worked at doing odd jobs, adding that my real work was peace work. When she prodded, I explained my vigils outside the gates. "Law," she said, slapping my knee, "we got us a Joshua here for sure. You just keep right on blowin' that horn, honey, one day them walls will come tumblin' down!" We had a good laugh.

I arrived before Walter and Elizabeth, who still aren't here. Jenine was busy making peach pies in the kitchen. I peeled the peaches while she rolled out the dough, and we had a brief chat, mostly about her work at the convent school. Father was watching television as usual, and as usual didn't seem very friendly, though we did talk about gardening for a bit. He used to put in all kinds of vegetables, but now he says he's too tired. A few cherry tomato plants and some parsley that came up from last year was all I saw. Mom came out on the porch and we sat together for a while. She doesn't look well but didn't want to talk about it, at least not around my father. Didn't want to deal with his fussing, I suppose.

I am curious to see Stephen, and Philip too, though Philip usually shies away from me in a way Stephen doesn't. Maybe it's a difference in how I relate to the two of them, I'm not sure. Sometimes Philip reminds me too much of Walter.

When Mom went in, I went for my usual walk, following the stream. I love this patch of woods; it's always cooler here. Found some stones Stephen might like. I'm curious about what his reaction will be to seeing me; it's been a while.

Received a letter before I left from Jim and Maureen in Kentucky. The commune has had a bumper crop this summer, not only of vegetables but of babies. Dan and Andrea had a little boy, and Marissa gave birth to twin girls three days later. Dan helped with Andrea's delivery and is bursting with pride to have "caught" his son. The twins were born in hospital. All three babies and their mothers are doing fine. Wish I were there to see them, but it will have to wait until this project is over. Jim promised to send pictures.

CHAPTER 7

▼

Elizabeth didn't sleep well that night. The diary had set her mind churning with politics, and weapons, and wars. What a terrible spring it had been! She was ashamed to admit that she hadn't been aware of half of it, except for Chernobyl, and even there she hadn't quite realized how appalling it was. She rarely watched television news unless there was a crisis, and even then, if it was upsetting, she frequently tuned out. She had discovered that if she did this for a few days news stories tended to disappear, demoted by the networks from crisis status to something you shouldn't waste energy worrying about. Libya, for example, would vanish from the television screen and be replaced by a famine somewhere, or a town devastated by flood. Television sometimes seemed to her like a giant eraser, like a teacher writing something on the blackboard but before you had a chance to copy it down, or even think about it, it was erased, and something else written on it instead. The process eventually lulled you into thinking that crises went away by themselves, that the problems somehow got solved without anybody having to do a thing: yet another way television falsified reality.

She was troubled too by other emotions the diary had stirred. She hadn't expected to be so touched by it. It hurt her to see how shut out from the family Henry felt, and the pain this gave him; he seemed to know so few other people. His courage, and his stubbornness, filled her with astonished admiration. She was also struck by his feelings for Jenine, and wondered if he wasn't half in love with her.

Her heart ached for his loneliness, and she didn't want it to. To give in to such feelings involved sliding still further down her imaginary hill, which she was earnestly trying not to do. She didn't need such complications in her life, she told herself; reading the diary had created a dangerous intimacy. She would send it back, with a note to him inside, and let that be the end of it.

But she could not get rid of the lure of curiosity, nor could she banish a surprising touch of jealousy. Was she angry at Henry for dreaming of Jenine rather than herself? That was absurd: if one were to spin a romantic tale, Jenine and Henry were much better suited to each other (like Ashley and Melanie in *Gone With The Wind*, she thought), than he could be with someone like her. Who but Jenine, having taken vows herself, could sympathize with the depth of his commitment to non-violence? To say nothing of their having shared the same complicated childhood.

Unfortunately for Henry, one of Jenine's vows (though they were not yet final) was a vow of chastity. Elizabeth couldn't imagine Jenine giving up her vocation and marrying, even if consanguinity or the differences in their ages posed no problem.

But what nonsense she was thinking! There was nothing to suggest that Jenine had any feelings for Henry other than what was proper for a niece, and Henry himself would be the first to deny that there was any sexual feeling between them. Indeed, if it hadn't been for that one diary entry recording a wet dream, she wouldn't have suspected Henry of any sexual feelings at all. They seemed thoroughly sublimated.

He loves Jenine the way he loved Sylvie, his sister, she thought. Elizabeth knew Sylvie only from the photographs she had seen in an album Mrs. Abbott had once showed her, which began with pictures of Sylvie as a baby and ended with one of her at nineteen, laughing into the camera, holding baby Jenine on her hip. Her hair was blonde, unlike Jenine's, but the resemblance between them was striking. Walter had been sixteen when Sylvie died; it had happened years before Elizabeth met him, but he had never wanted to talk about it. None of the family did; yet sometimes, in a curious way, it seemed as if Sylvie was always there in the background, like a barely acknowledged ghost.

She stirred restlessly, thinking about the Abbotts and the effects of Sylvie's death, the ripples and circles that spread out over time as they did when water was disturbed by a stone. Had it partly determined what Henry had chosen to become? Was it Sylvie's death that made Walter more or less shut down emotionally, or had he been that way from childhood? She had never felt comfortable asking Mrs. Abbott such questions. Without being told, she knew they were taboo.

The effect of her death on Mrs. Abbott was clear enough: Walter had commented several times how different his mother had been before his sister died.

Perhaps it had been the dual loss, of their mother as they had always known her as well as their sister, that so affected her brothers.

She turned over, thumping the pillow into a new shape. It was depressing to think how a chance event could be the cause of so much pain, that its echoes could travel so far. She gathered that the family had been a basically happy one until Sylvie's accident.

Walter, beside her, had settled into a steady snore. She jostled him with her foot to make him stop, then reached for the sleep-aid pills the pharmacist had suggested. She unscrewed the cap, groped in the darkness for her water glass, and swallowed two.

*   *   *   *

The next day she busied herself with housework, determined to put Henry out of her mind. She did three loads of laundry, and in a burst of ecological virtue lugged them outside to the back yard and hung them up to dry instead of throwing them in the dryer. It was something she hadn't done in years, since childhood, in fact, when she used to help her mother hang out the clothes, taking the items out of the basket one by one and shaking them before handing them to her mother to pin on the line. She had never really enjoyed this chore, particularly in the winter when her wet mittens would get cold and stiff, but to her surprise she now found it rather fun. The fresh smell of the clothes was a delight, and it was a challenge to hang them up just so, the sheets at either end balancing the shorts and socks and jeans in the middle. Pleased with herself, and grateful to the previous owners of the house for having strung up the clothesline, she went inside to vacuum.

Thirty minutes later she was reminded why clothes dryers were such a successful invention. The sun, overtaken by clouds, vanished; it started to rain, which turned within minutes into a downpour. She had to scramble to take everything off the line and drag the basket, much heavier now that the clothes were sodden, down to the basement.

The boys were leaving for summer camp in two days, where they'd be until August. After vacuuming, she sat down to make a list of the things she needed to pack, putting at the top *two flashlights*, an item she had forgotten the previous year. When the clothes were done, she put in another load, folding and sorting the dry ones. Then she started sewing name tapes on seven pairs each of socks and shirts and underwear. By the time she finished and fixed herself lunch, the sun was out again. She decided to go for a walk, and stop at the library.

It was a small, volunteer library, housed on two floors of an old brick building that must once have been someone's home. She walked up the polished wooden stairs to the adult section. The books were mostly romance novels by outdated authors like Louis Bromfield and Daphne du Maurier, their covers stained, their pages yellowing. Non-fiction included hoary "psychology" books like *How To Make Friends and Influence People* and volumes on gardening and crafts. To her surprise, there were two books on vegetarian cooking, which was what she was looking for. She took both of them, and from the New Fiction shelf a novel called *The Handmaid's Tale* by a Canadian, Margaret Atwood.

It crossed her mind that if she wanted to avoid a quarrel with Walter, she would have to read the cookbooks in secret. Possibly the Margaret Atwood too— from the blurb on the back cover she gathered it was something of a feminist tract. Maybe she should ask at the desk to have all of them wrapped in plain brown paper, she thought, and giggled.

From the library it was an easy walk to the pharmacy in the mall to pick up a new set of nail clippers for Walter, who'd lost his, and some Tylenol for Philip, who was complaining recently of pains in his legs. On impulse, she also purchased a steno notebook. The way it was designed, she noticed, hadn't changed since high school—the same blue-lined pages with a light red line running down the center, bound at the top with a metal coil. She had taken two years of shorthand in high school, which she had, in fact, been pretty good at. Her father had insisted she take it "so she'd always have something to fall back on," an agenda she had fought at the time (she had no intention of spending her life as a secretary in some man's office), but which turned out to be the one useful thing she remembered learning in high school. Being able to take her university class notes in shorthand not only enabled her to get most of the lectures down for later transcription and study, but it had the added advantage of making the notes impossible for anyone to borrow. It was also fun to see what percentage of the professor's words you could capture, a challenge that had enlivened many otherwise dull classes. If she kept a diary, she thought, she would write it in shorthand. No one in the family would be able to read it, unless they had the Rosette stone, which was highly unlikely: no one studied Gregg shorthand any more.

But did she really *want* to keep a diary? She had never done so, not even as a child. The thought was vaguely disquieting: what would she say to herself in a diary? And what if she discovered she had nothing to say, that her thoughts were trivial, dull? It would be humiliating. And what might happen if she put her darkest thoughts on paper, uncensored by concern for how the children would hear it, or Walter? Her diary wouldn't be reflections on world affairs, like

Henry's, but an expression of her feelings for the people around her. She assumed she would be honest, particularly if the diary were written in indecipherable shorthand, but honesty, even with one's self, had its dangers, did it not? There was an aura of narcissistic self-absorption about it she distrusted. It was questionable whether diary-keeping alleviated loneliness, for example, or sharpened it, whether it was an aide to ridding oneself of discontent or an encouragement to wallow in it.

She was making an absurd fuss about nothing, she thought as she let herself in the house: just because she had bought a steno pad didn't mean she had to write in it. She could use it for grocery lists, or messages.

After dinner the four of them played a prolonged game of Monopoly, which Walter won. As they were putting the money and cards away, Elizabeth casually asked Stephen and Philip if either of them had received any classes on drugs in school the previous term.

Both boys nodded. "Just before the year stopped, they showed us a video," Philip said. "It was scary. It was about all these babies jerking and twitching because their mothers smoked crack."

Those babies again: she might have guessed. "You've never heard of anyone in your school trying crack, have you?" she asked, looking carefully at both of them.

"No, ma'am," Stephen answered. "There's some who smoke grass. They'd probably smoke crack if they could, but I don't think they sell it around here. Anyway, we know enough not to try it, you shouldn't worry."

Elizabeth, relieved, kissed them goodnight and sent them up to bed. She watched television with Walter for a while, then took a bath and read Margaret Atwood until she fell asleep.

*   *   *   *

The week passed. She had no contact with Henry, but neither could she keep from thinking of him. She and Walter drove the boys up to Pennsylvania to Camp Manitou, saw them safely ensconced in their respective cabins, and drove back home to an empty house, though it was only truly empty when Walter was at work and Elizabeth had it to herself. She enjoyed the solitude, but found it hard to find enough things to occupy her. She finished the Margaret Atwood novel, which was amusing but a bit strained, in her opinion, what her mother would have called "far-fetched." She read through the cook books she had taken from the library, putting a discrete pencil check by recipes that looked promising, and then spent one rainy afternoon copying them onto note cards.

She listened to the radio as she did these things, not to the classical music station she normally listened to, but one with talking heads so that their voices would pre-empt her own thoughts. Arts talk shows were good for this, she discovered, or "All Things Considered" on National Public Radio. In the evenings she and Walter watched television, or had friends over for dinner and bridge. During those occasions she drank too much wine, chattered too volubly, and made love to Walter. She took up knitting, starting with a simple angora scarf. She tried several of the recipes she had copied down.

On Thursday she called the Zen center and told them she wouldn't be coming in that evening. Sitting for an hour with nothing but her own thoughts for company struck her as too risky. She had no faith that she could keep her distance from them, that it would not turn into a combat, with the thoughts of Henry winning.

She grew increasingly restless, and considered going to Baltimore to visit her sister; she even at one point had her hand on the dial to phone her, but then thought better of it. Linda didn't like things that were "complicated" or "unpleasant." She was not likely to understand or sympathize with Elizabeth's malaise; she would probably consider her attraction to Henry scandalous, if not simply tacky. Her predictable advice, which Elizabeth didn't want to hear, would be to put Henry from mind, seek counseling, consult her doctor, all good, sensible stuff she wasn't in the mood for. Even if it turned out that she ended following such advice, she didn't want to hear it from her sister.

Sometimes Elizabeth wondered if sisters ever forgave each other for not being the sisters they secretly wanted. A part of her was still angry at the lack of intimacy between Linda and herself, angry that Linda had grown up to be someone she didn't want to be intimate with. Her sister, the prom queen. All those ball gowns in high school, all those gardenias.

Once past puberty Linda had played completely by the rules, looking down her disapproving nose at hippies like Elizabeth, who turned seventeen in 1967, when Mick Jagger and the Stones were encouraging sympathy for the Devil. Gardenias, to Elizabeth, were anathema. She wore jeans or Indian wrap-around skirts, beaded Indian earrings; she despised formality, and fled anything resembling ritualized male/female games, which seemed to her to demean everyone involved.

Playing by the rules had worked well for Linda, she reflected. She had been happily married for fourteen years now, thank you very much, to her handsome heart surgeon husband, whose profession was beyond reproach. No feeling awkward for Linda when someone asked what her husband did for a living, not the shadow of a qualm. Totally happy in her big house with its landscaped grounds, happy with their vacations in Acapulco, their luxury cars. No, she would not go to Baltimore.

She didn't call her friend Arlene either, not wanting to explain why she was skipping the Zen workshop. She didn't want to share her feelings with anyone, as if hearing herself say out loud that she was disturbed or confused or unhappy risked giving it a greater importance than it deserved. As long as it remained unspoken, she could still think of her preoccupation with Henry as mere fantasy, something possible to dismiss, something under control.

For the same reason the pages of the steno notebook remained blank.

*   *   *   *

Jenine was leaving the school playground, her hand on the gate of the metal fence that led to the sidewalk, when two men wearing gray suits and hats suddenly appeared in front of her. The first touched his hat brim with one hand and with the other took an identity card bearing his picture out of his breast pocket. "Excuse me, ma'am," he said smoothly, "we are agents from Internal Security at Fort Detrick. We have a few questions you might be able to help us with concerning a gentleman named Henry Abbott. He is, I believe, your uncle?"

Jenine nodded, her heart quickening at the mention of Henry's name. She had never been questioned before by anyone with a badge. Was Henry in trouble?

"We won't take but a minute of your time, ma'am, this is just a routine check," the other man put in. "We are concerned about Mr. Abbott's whereabouts this past weekend, specifically on the days of July 4th and July 5th. Would you by any chance be able to verify where he was at that time?"

"Is Henry is some sort of trouble?" Jenine asked. "Is there something wrong at Fort Detrick?"

"No, ma'am," the first man replied. "Like we said, this is just a routine check. Can you testify to Mr. Abbott's whereabouts on those days?"

"Yes I can, and so can the rest of his family," Jenine said tartly. "He was with all of us at his parents' farm for the entire weekend. Please, I hope you aren't going to worry them with questions like this," she said anxiously, "Mother Abbott isn't well."

"No, ma'am, your word will be enough," the second man said with a pleasant smile. "That's all we needed to know, and we thank you for your time." With a slight bow and a final tip of their hats, the two of them moved on down the street.

Jenine stood where she was, uncertain what to do. The encounter was obscurely frightening, though for all she knew, keeping tabs on dissidents like Henry was, as they said, routine. The idea was astonishing. From their dress and demeanor she might have mistaken the men for Mormons doing their visiting duties or Jehovah's Witnesses distributing copies of *The Watchtower,* certainly not government agents sent to check up on dissidents, or suspected law-breakers. Henry had done nothing illegal, she was sure; whatever suspicions they might have of him were unfounded.

She wondered if their visit had been intended to frighten him in a roundabout way, or whether something had happened in the labs at Fort Detrick over the 4th of July weekend—something gone missing, perhaps, Top Secret documents, or a vial of something. If so, "subversives" like Henry would naturally be on the list of suspects. She paused to wonder if she agreed with that. If there was credible evidence that such a theft posed a threat, the men's questions shouldn't be considered harassment but prudence: a single terrorist incident at Fort Detrick, after all, could have consequences too terrible to think about.

It worried her that she couldn't tell which it was, and that there was no way, with all the government secrecy, that she could find out why they wanted to know Henry's whereabouts on the 4th of July. She decided that in any case she should let Henry know about the men's visit. Had he himself been questioned, she wondered, was he aware that military security people were monitoring his movements and tracking down his relatives for questioning? She felt in her pocket for her keys. She should go back in and call him from the school phone, but she hesitated. If Henry was under government surveillance, his phone could possibly be tapped. She wouldn't want the school to be involved.

She opened the gate and stepped out on the sidewalk. She would call from the Mother House, she decided, or even better, from a public phone. She shivered slightly at the strangeness of this new way of thinking, as if she was engaging in something clandestine. She felt, for the first time she could remember, *observed;* and by agents of her own government. Who knew what they were capable of, or how far they would go? She didn't believe this incident was serious, but she felt uneasy, and somehow curiously ashamed, as if simply knowing you were under surveillance made you suspect yourself of having done something wrong. People in Germany during Hitler's time must have felt a bit like this, she thought, or people in Russia or China. She shivered at the strangeness of it. This was *America;* one didn't fear one's government in America.

It then occurred to her that she would be doing Henry no favor in telling him, that knowing for sure that he was being watched by federal agents might make him suspect everyone, turn him paranoid. Maybe that's what the government wanted, so they could then discredit him as a crazy person. She shouldn't tell him of the security detail. But surely he would want to know?

She located a public phone booth and searched for his name in the directory. It wasn't there, even though she went through the listings for every village in the vicinity. Perhaps he had an unlisted phone, though more likely he had no phone at all; it occurred to her, belatedly, that it was probably a luxury he couldn't afford. She would have to write him. She didn't know his address, but Mrs. Abbott would have it.

She walked back to the Mother House, lost in thought. By the time she began helping with dinner preparations, however, the idea of calling Mrs. Abbott didn't seem such a good one. She didn't want to worry her, to say nothing of Henry's father, and she couldn't think of a way to explain why she needed Henry's address without telling a lie. She wondered if Elizabeth would have it. It was possible, though she would have to wait to call until Monday when Walter was at work and she could be certain he wouldn't answer the phone. Somehow she didn't think Henry would want his brother knowing about the investigation before he did.

Though perhaps Walter already knew, she thought, surely he too had been questioned? But if so, why would they need her to verify Henry's whereabouts on the 4th of July? She sighed; it would be nice to have been born into a less complicated family, or live in a less complicated world. She would call Elizabeth on Monday. Henry could spend the rest of the weekend worry-free.

After dinner and devotions, she retired to her room. It had been a tiring day, not helped by the fact that her period was due any time. She had felt uncoordinated and clumsy all afternoon, and the children had seemed especially boisterous. There had been good things in the day too, of course, Candace, her favorite among the girls, giving her an impish smile after reciting the poem she had written about her kitten; Larry, in the second grade class, so pleased with himself for playing well in dodge ball. But it had all been overshadowed by the men in gray. That's how she thought of them, the men in gray: a blend of black and white, ambiguous, in between good and evil.

She undressed and knelt beside the bed, asking God for forgiveness for her fears, and for guidance as to what to tell Henry. She prayed for him, and for her grandparents, and for the sisters she lived with at the Mother House. She prayed for her government to act with wisdom, for countries to peacefully resolve their differences. Please God, she prayed, let the shadow of war be lifted from us, so that children will not be harmed.

As she climbed into bed she remembered Sister Amalie telling her last winter about the way the Catholics at Jonah House had marked the Feast of the Innocents. They had held an all-night prayer vigil at the Pentagon, led by Daniel and Philip Berrigan, after which, at dawn, two Catholic laymen and a nun poured a ceremonial vial of their blood on the steps. They were arrested, as they expected to be, each receiving two-year prison sentences for "defiling government property."

There had been about thirty people at the vigil. No cameras, of course: the crowds weren't large enough, Sister Amalie said, and the government didn't want such actions publicized, they were afraid it might make the Catholic protest movement grow.

Jenine had been slightly shocked at Sister Amalie for telling her this. She didn't know what to think of the Berrigans. She had been moved by one of Father Philip's poems that she read in an anthology in high school, but their actions against draft boards during the Vietnam war, and most recently, against missile bases, seemed to her extreme. She didn't know what to think of her cousin Henry's daily protest at Edgewood Arsenal either, though heaven knows his vigil was much milder than the things the Jonah House people engaged in. She reminded herself that they were Catholics, and deeply committed to their faith. She admired them for that, as well as for their courage, but the idea of going to jail horrified her. She wasn't brave, she knew that. She prayed every night to be strong of heart like the early Christians, while silently hoping that she would never have to undergo anything like their persecution and suffering: she doubted how strong her faith would be if it was tested in the extreme.

All her life she had shrunk from any involvement in politics. Politics involved conflict, and taking sides; it involved making judgments she didn't feel qualified to make. She had always taken refuge in the thought that she was too young to have political views; she didn't know enough about the world, she hadn't lived long enough. The best she could do, she thought, was try to do good to those around her, the children she taught, her sisters at the Mother House, her family.

It struck her that she didn't see any of her family members nearly as often as she should. She wrote letters every week to her grandparents, but in between occasions like Christmas and the Fourth of July, she had little or no contact with them, or with either of her uncles, or Elizabeth. That should change, she thought. Perhaps it would when she called Elizabeth for Henry's address. She had felt very warm toward Elizabeth when they watched the fireworks together, much like she imagined real sisters would be. They might not be able to see each other very often, her duties at the Mother House didn't allow for being away except during official holidays, and some of those were taken up with retreats. But they could correspond. The Church might be too poor for Greyhound tickets, but it could afford postage stamps.

She closed her eyes and snuggled down to sleep, to dream that she was walking barefoot on a pebble beach beside the ocean. She glanced at the water and was startled to see that with each wave the ocean was retreating, exposing more and more dry land. She turned, frightened, and began walking towards the forested hill behind her. The path climbed steeply upwards, and it was pebbly, but it was a relief from the painful sharpness of the stones on the shore that had bruised her feet. She climbed upward, hopeful, but once at the top of the hill she found herself surrounded by an immense slag heap filled with giant pieces of concrete that jutted from the ground like knives, as if a highway had been torn up and dumped here.

It was growing dark. She had to pick her way among the jagged rocks, placing her feet with care. The ground began to slope downwards, and she inched forward, feeling with her toes. Suddenly a flash of color off to her left caught her eye. She turned to examine it, and discovered, half-hidden in the crevice of a boulder, a single perfect daffodil. She drew in her breath sharply. The flower seemed to be pulsing with a miraculous light. She found herself peering directly into its throat. She could see every detail of its petals, the tiny bluish veins, the lacy frill of the cup surrounding the stamens. And then she went deeper still, into the vulva, which pulsed with a warm, golden light. She gazed at it in wonder, till it faded, and it grew too dark to see.

She didn't know how long she slept, but it was still totally dark when she woke to the sensation of wetness between her legs. Hurriedly she turned on the light, which confirmed her fear. Her period had come, there was blood on her nightdress, blood on her sheets. She stuffed some tissue between her legs and went to the cupboard where she kept her belt and sanitary pads. What a nuisance: the sheets had just been changed the day before. She sighed. Another of God's little challenges, as Sister Roseanne would say, which should be met with prayer. *Hail Mary full of grace blessed art thou among women,* she thought as she fumbled with the straps of her belt, and blessed is the fruit of thy womb, Jesus, but her mind was drugged with sleep, and fruit of the womb turned into fruit of the loom, which was the advertisement for sheets and linens she used to see in her grandmother's magazines….

There, the pad was secure. She would deal with the sheets at matins. Forgive me, Father, she prayed, and crawled back into the warmth of the bed.

CHAPTER 8

▼

The following Saturday Elizabeth and Walter had a serious fight. It seemed to her he had been restless and irritable all day, complaining of the heat, complaining that he hadn't been able to find the tools he needed to mend the Venetian blind in the study, some metal part of which had snapped off. He had been morose all through dinner (which was pasta and chicken cacciatore, not vegetarian, so that couldn't have been the cause). As she was clearing the dishes away, it occurred to Elizabeth to suggest they go to a film. It might lighten his mood, she thought, and hers too; if they hurried they could catch the early show. She threw on a clean blouse and they rushed out, before she had a chance to check the paper to see what was playing.

It turned out to be a film called *Aliens*, which she hated. Halfway through she had suggested to Walter that they leave, but he had refused. She shouldn't take it seriously, he said, it was only a film.

It chilled her that he seemed actually to be enjoying it. To her it was a revolting melange of ugly computer-generated images: grotesque, swollen insect-like creatures with death's heads, oozing acid drool through serrated needle-sharp teeth, other creatures equipped with octopus-like tentacles and the ability to leap and fly like lizards, or bats. Or were these the same creatures? She couldn't tell; their ugliness so revolted her she kept closing her eyes.

She stayed to see how much worse it could get. She stayed grimly, gritting her teeth, her outrage and revulsion growing with each interminable scene, each new inexplicable explosion accompanied by the shrill shrieks of the dying aliens as they were blown to pieces and hurled into space, all in lurid color, like some vicious, animated Hieronymus Bosch, except with a deafening sound track. She hated the way the film seemed to exploit every known female fear: the terror of being imprisoned—"cocooned," as they called it, trapped alive in some sticky hardened mucous, like a pupae, awaiting impregnation by aliens. The terror of rape, in the scene where one of them attacks Sigourney Weaver and wraps its tentacles around her throat; the fear of being impregnated by a monster rapist and giving birth to something too horrible to look at. But the scenes that most appalled her were the "birth" scenes, when some horrible bloody lump would appear in the victim's chest and after a hideous parody of labor a grotesque alien shape would suddenly erupt, in the process tearing the "mother" to pieces. Did this film maker hate the birth process, she wondered? Who would loathe women enough to want to put such horrible images in their heads? Was he ignorant, this director, was he sick, or was he terminally cynical about the violence of his images?

She fidgeted in her seat, she fumed. Why did theaters distribute films like this, why did people pay to see them? That they made you *pay* for such ugliness seemed the crowning insult. You had no one to blame but yourself, for no one had forced you to come here: you were here voluntarily, *caveat emptor*. She should walk out, she thought, she should demand her money back; but that would be considered "making a scene," which as Walter's wife she wasn't allowed to do, unless she wanted it talked about all over town.

Every now and then she turned her eyes from the screen and stared at Walter. The sight of him chewing away at his popcorn, absorbed in the film, made her cringe. Again she thought of getting up and leaving: she could drive home and pick him up later, when it was over; she could wait in a restaurant, have a coffee. But she didn't; she sat where she was, rigid with dislike. The ending seemed to drag on forever—the monster mother had to be killed again and again, at tedious length. There had to be multiple fires, multiple Armored Personnel Carrier races, threats of imminent nuclear explosions.

The little girl, of course, is rescued, emerging from these multiple traumas without a single scar, not even a psychological one. Mother Sigourney fights like a superhero, with grenade launchers and flame throwers, to save her from the evil mother Alien, at one point battling inside an armored forklift and gallumphing around in ten-ton boots. At the climax, she hurls the monster into deep space. The image of Female as Rambo grafted onto the idea of a wrathful mother tiger, to say nothing of The Female As Incubator Of Monsters If Not Rescued by the Marines was loathsome.

She was so angry by the time they left the theater that she flew at Walter even before they settled into the car. "How can you have enjoyed that appalling piece of trash?" she demanded. "You did enjoy it, I know you did, I was watching, and in some places you were actually *smiling*."

"Oh for heaven's sake, Elizabeth, why not?" Walter drawled. "I didn't go in expecting William Shakespeare. Of course it was trash, all horror films are, but it was entertaining, rather well-put together trash. It's not supposed to be taken seriously, you know, any more than the Saturday afternoon cliff-hangers we used to go to as kids. Did you get all worked up about those too?"

"Those cliff-hangers were never as obscenely manipulative as this film, and you know it," she retorted. "The images were revolting. They demeaned the birth process, demeaned women in all kinds of ways. Surely you saw that?"

"No, frankly, I didn't. I should think it could be equally argued that in a quirky kind of way, it was trying to be a feminist film."

"A *feminist* film," she echoed incredulously. "Good lord, what kind of feminism are you talking about? That we'll all be equal Rambo's together, toting huge phallic grenade launchers?"

"Oh for God's sake, Elizabeth, don't make a thing of it: it was just a film. I'm sorry you didn't like it, but I'm not in the mood for arguments about feminism."

He parked the car in the drive and they went into the house. She sat down on the sofa, still angry, and grew angrier when he handed her a drink: he hadn't asked if she wanted one, and it was bourbon on ice, which she'd told him many times before she didn't like. She set it down. "It's not enough to say it's 'just a film'," she objected. "Don't you see how films like this affect people? Children, for example, *our* children. How much do they learn about men's attitudes toward women from the films they see? They probably spend as much time watching film stars as they do watching us. And what kind of female image are young girls supposed to get from Sigourney Weaver's bulging biceps?"

"Oh surely that's a parody," Walter replied. "It's a spoof of Sylvester Stallone. Besides, I should imagine a young girl in a single-parent household might feel more secure protected by a mother with large biceps. The central aspect of Ripley's character is that she's a mother, after all; she fights to save her child. Why do you think the kid called herself Newt, by the way? Did I hear that right?"

Elizabeth ignored his question. "It's not a spoof," she said, "the film is a covert glorification of violence in women, conferring on it a Seal of Approval. In the name of equality, in the name of *motherhood,* for god's sake, it says we'll all be warriors together in the great American future, equal in throwing our lethal weapons around. Films like this pretend to be a spoof of the Rambo mentality when they're really propagandizing for it. It's their way of having it both ways. I hate it."

Walter lit a cigarette. "You're being a touch hysterical, don't you think, Scarlet?" He yawned. "I'm a bit tired; how about let's going up to bed and fighting it out up there? We'd have a better chance of reaching accommodation, don't you think?" He winked, which looked to her unpleasantly like a leer. "Did you turn the air conditioning on, by the way, before we left?" he asked.

"No," she returned sharply, "did you?" She was the one who usually took care of such details, but there was no law that she should always be the one to do it. And air-conditioning was hardly the point. It was infuriating that he should change the subject like this, as if the conversation was of no importance, and whatever she might have to say on the subject even less so. The lascivious wink and the suggestion that a good fuck would pacify her was the last straw.

Walter looked at her quizzically. "Sorry, I assumed you had turned it on, you usually do," he said mildly. He swallowed the rest of his drink and put out his cigarette, his signal that the conversation was over. "I'll go up and do it," he said, "maybe take a shower. Are you coming?"

"No, I'm not," Elizabeth answered.

"You mean you'll be up later?" he asked.

She said nothing. She didn't even look at him, not until he stood up to go. When she spoke her voice was flat, and uncharacteristically firm. "No," she said, "I mean I won't be coming at all. I'll be sleeping in the boys' room tonight."

She had never said such a thing before; they had not slept apart while under the same roof since their wedding. It was a major breach, and Walter stared at it blankly for a full minute, uncomprehending. Then he grasped what she was saying and his manner changed. "And pray why will you be doing that?" he mocked. "Because we have different views about a film I'm to be denied my conjugal rights, and you deprived of yours?"

She flushed, her anger momentarily swallowed by amazement at his effrontery. When crossed, Walter was capable of behaving like a spiteful child, like that hateful dwarf Rumplestiltskin in the fairy tale, tearing his beard and stamping his feet. Not that he ever physically lost control: instead he used sneers, and cold, sarcastic logic. She returned his stare, unblinking, and suddenly saw many things, all at once and with shocking clarity, among them the certainty that she could not continue living with this man.

The awareness made her dizzy. She didn't recognize the person thinking such thoughts. The situation seemed unreal; Walter seemed unreal. She took a swallow of her drink, trying to shake the incredulity that was spreading to encompass not only their present but their past, indeed, the whole of their life together. How could she have lived with this man all these years and not seen who he was? She had borne two children to someone she barely knew. She gripped the arm of the sofa and took a swallow of her drink. "We'll talk about all this tomorrow," she said stonily, "I can't be civil at the moment. Goodnight."

She set down her glass and went upstairs, without looking at him. She carried her nightgown and robe into Stephen's room, together with a glass of water and two valerian pills. She closed the door and carefully locked it. The gesture was unnecessary, Walter's pride would never allow him to use force, but the click of the lock pleased her. It was like a small echo of Ibsen's Norah slamming the door: it made her feel powerful. Like Sigourney Weaver, she thought sourly, and reached for the light.

She lay in the darkness, turning over in her mind the idea of living alone. What it would be like to sleep in a single bed again, like this one she was lying on? It would have its good points (no elbows jabbing you in the middle of the night, no snores), but it would also be difficult. It would be lonely. And then there were the children, but she couldn't think about their rights just now, it made things too complicated; it would confuse what was right for *her*. She would waver if she thought about them.

Lying there, alone, her explosion at Walter seemed melodramatic. What on earth had gotten into her? It was, after all, just a film, a trivial thing to quarrel about when you thought about it. Was she, as Walter so frequently claimed, "over-reacting"? Maybe her hormones were messed up, and her period coming early was a sign.

They had quarreled like this before, with Walter accusing her of being hysterical and she seeing him as bloodless, like a fish but more calculating. The quarrels had never been resolved but put out of sight in order to keep the peace. Until tonight they always ended with her capitulation, with her shutting her eyes to what she always secretly knew, which was that at bottom she despised this man. This time she was determined to hold onto the perception. It was the heart's truth.

*   *   *   *

The next day neither spoke of what had happened. Walter took the car without telling her where he was going, only that he'd be back for dinner. When he returned, they were mutually silent. After serving his meal, she went back upstairs to Stephen's room.

On Monday, as she was putting the breakfast things in the dishwasher, Jenine called, asking if by chance she had Henry's address. She did, though only by chance, only because it was written in the fly leaf of the diary. Walter had already left for work; she retrieved the notebook from its hiding place in the shoe bag in her closet and hurried back to the phone.

"Doesn't Henry have a telephone, Jenine?" she asked when she picked up the receiver, though she vaguely remembered his telling her that he didn't.

"I don't think he can afford one," Jenine answered, "or maybe he doesn't have one on principle, I don't know." She paused, thinking, *maybe he thinks if he had a phone it would be tapped.*

"Sorry to be nosy, but why do you want his address?" Elizabeth inquired.

Jenine explained about the security agents stopping her at school and asking about Henry's whereabouts on July 4th. She thought Henry should know, she said, it worried her. "Has anyone contacted you?" she asked. "Have you ever been questioned about Henry?"

"No, never," Elizabeth said. Jenine's news was disconcerting. Henry had been doing his non-violent witness at Edgewood for almost a year; why should they be asking questions about him now? She thought rapidly. If anyone had interrogated Walter about his brother, surely he would have mentioned it. "Do you know if anyone has called Mr. or Mrs. Abbott?" she asked.

"I don't think so, and I don't think they will; they said my word would be enough. I thought of calling Mother Abbott for Henry's address, but I knew I'd have to explain why and I didn't want to worry her. Isn't it strange, Elizabeth, do you think something is going on at Fort Detrick?"

"If there is, I'd be the last to know about it, I'm sure," Elizabeth said tartly. "Even if Walter knows, it's against the law for him to talk about it to me."

"I know. Okay then. I've already written the letter to Henry, I'll mail it to him this afternoon." She paused, adding, "You do think I'm right to do this, Elizabeth, don't you, that I'm not worrying him unnecessarily?"

"Of course you're right," Elizabeth said, "I mean, wouldn't you want to know if you were he?"

Jenine hesitated. "In one way, no, not really; I think I'd rather stay ignorant. But in the long run, I suppose, yes. Knowledge in this case seems a necessary evil." She sighed, and when Elizabeth didn't immediately answer, thanked her and said good-bye.

Elizabeth frowned and put the receiver down. Jenine hadn't seemed comfortable talking on the phone; the conversation was hurried, her voice had sounded strained. It occurred to her that perhaps she thought their phone might be bugged. The idea brought her up short. Was it?

It was the first time she had considered the possibility. She realized she had no idea whether it was or not, nor had she any idea how to find out. It seemed logical enough that it would be, particularly if "something was going on" at Fort Detrick, in which case they might want to be keeping close tabs on employees like Walter. Because of his relationship with Henry, Walter was probably considered a security risk. If, for example, some secret formula for whatever they were putting together in the weapons labs had gone missing—or worse, a bomb's worth of chemicals had been stolen, there would be heightened security checks on all employees, including those who had been already cleared.

She had always understood this, even believed it was reasonable to have a law forbidding husbands to talk to their wives about what they did at work. After all, with her "hippie" past (and perhaps also her foreign birth), how could the government be sure she wouldn't some day leak information to someone who could, in turn, leak it to the Russians? From their point of view, she was a potential security risk; and she had to admit that their suspicions weren't completely unreasonable. Who knows under what circumstances she would tell what she knew to some group working to curb the arms race? It was fortunate that she knew precious little, and no more than what could be found in Henry's pamphlets. Her ignorance protected her.

She poured herself another cup of coffee, stirring in a teaspoon of sugar, thinking of Jenine's phrase, "necessary evil," which is how secrecy was seen by the government. But it was an evil created by a prior, more primal evil, which was the making of weapons so horrible that they had to be kept secret from "the enemy" lest he take it in his head to build some himself. Kept secret too, conveniently, from the taxpayers, who didn't really want to know the consequences to flesh and blood of using such weapons, and were only too happy to be kept in the dark.

She thought of Jenine's decision to tell Henry what she knew, and whether she herself should tell Walter of Jenine's call. She turned on the radio for the mid-day report, half-hoping to hear news of some incident at Fort Detrick which would make the decision for her. There was nothing, of course. She took her cup to the sink and washed it slowly, staring out the window. If she held her tongue, she would be adding Jenine's call to the pile of other unspoken things she carried around that she saw no point talking to Walter about. On the other hand, if something suspicious was going on at Detrick, it certainly dwarfed their quarrel over a film, or even what was happening to their marriage. She felt vaguely frightened. Yes, she would probably leave Walter, she thought, but some day, not in the immediate future. Not this week.

She wondered if she would be able to detect anything in Walter's posture or the way he spoke—*if* he spoke, that is, which he would if she apologized and called a truce. It also occurred to her to wonder if he felt as stifled as she by all the things he wasn't allowed to say. On any level, government or personal, secrets stifled. They warped.

Which didn't prevent her from deciding in the end not to tell Walter of Jenine's call. She didn't want a truce, not at least until she had a chance to talk about Jenine's news to Henry, and she couldn't do this until after Jenine's letter reached him. If it was mailed today, he should receive it by Friday. On Friday, she decided, she would go see him. She would go to his apartment and return the diary; seeing him might clarify things. Until then she would remain civil with Walter, and sleep in Stephen's room.

CHAPTER 9

▼

Though she watched Walter closely for the next three days, she could find nothing in his manner to suggest there was heightened security at Fort Detrick. In fact, Walter seemed more relaxed than usual. This might be partly pose, but she suspected it was also due to the arrival of the exercise machine he had ordered from a catalogue. He had set it up in the basement, together with their old television set, so he could watch baseball games or CNN while he exercised. He had spent every evening down there since it came.

At dinner, and during the time they shared watching television, he was civil, even entertaining. They were speaking to each other again, though not about anything important, their interaction more a mask of normalcy than the thing itself. Neither of them had as yet alluded to their quarrel over *Alien* or to Elizabeth's continued absence from the master bedroom; in consequence, every sentence that passed between them seemed to have a hole in it. It was as if they were engaged in a silent contest to see who would first drop the pretense and bring up the unspoken. For the moment, it was a stalemate.

On Friday she drove to the address written at the back of Henry's diary, tucking the small ringed notebook in the inside compartment of her purse. The house he lived in was at the end of a road that badly needed repaving, in a section of town she had never seen before. It was an old wooden house that looked, when she got out of the car, to be listing; it seemed canted to the right. She followed a short, overgrown path to the side entrance, looking for number 21-B, which suddenly appeared above a cement stair well. She walked down the steps and knocked on the door. The walls surrounding her smelled of dampness, but at least it was cool. There was no answer. She knocked again.

"Who is it?" Henry called from the other side.

"Elizabeth," she answered, "your sister-in-law," and wondered that she chose to identify herself that way.

When the door opened, she stepped in. Henry turned on the light and they hugged each other briefly. Oddly, though he seemed pleased to see her, he didn't seem surprised. He led her though a narrow hall and offered her some tea, as if he had known she was coming. "I've only home-grown chamomile," he said, "I hope you like it." He gestured her to the one chair in the room, an old painted oak upright that stood guard over a tiny table.

"I do, it's my mother's favorite; she grows it too," Elizabeth replied, adding, "Is it okay if I look around?"

She heard the words and blushed, realizing after she'd said them that they might be misconstrued as sarcasm. For there was nothing to see in Henry's apartment. In fact, it resembled a monk's cell, consisting of one small room, a bathroom, and a kitchenette. It was obvious from the single tiny black table and the solitary chair beside it that Henry rarely if ever had company. There was a small, battered-looking television set in one corner. Aside from the table and chair there was no other furniture, unless you counted the mattress on the floor beneath the window, neatly covered with a gray Army surplus blanket, on either side of which were two upright orange crates. These held neatly folded sweaters and T-shirts on their lower shelves, with a few books on top of one and a chess set on the other, laid out as if ready for a game. She wondered how much time Henry spent playing it, matching wits with himself.

In practice, "looking around" meant examining the books on top of the left-hand orange crate while Henry busied himself at the stove. There was a volume on organic gardening, two pamphlets by Caesar Chavez, a book on Sufism, a health food cook book, and something called *Studies in the Psychology of Zen*. Aside from the cook book and the Chavez pamphlets, they were all, she noticed, from the Baltimore library. She wondered how often he went there, and if he saw Jenine when he was in the city. Then she noticed that although the books were from the library, they had a small price sticker at the bottom of their back covers, which meant they were remainders, old books the library sold now and then for twenty-five or fifty cents to clear the shelves and make room for new. The due date stamped in the Zen book was 1980, six years ago.

She sat back down on the chair. Where did he keep his clothes, she wondered; T-shirts were in the orange crates, but where did he put his socks and underwear, even if he didn't own a suit? In a box in a closet? She didn't see any closets.

Maybe there was one in the hall; she hadn't noticed. Or maybe he had as few clothes as he seemed to have of everything else.

Initially the emptiness of the room had startled her, but by the time Henry came to the table with the teapot and two mugs, she had begun rather to like its spareness. She was pleased to find him so all of a piece, that his non-violence and voluntary simplicity came in a single package. On the other hand, the severity of his living arrangements was a bit extreme. There didn't appear to be any sugar, for example, or spoons to stir it with if there were. She refrained from asking, though the tea tasted bitter.

"I'm sorry, I don't have any sugar," Henry said. "Does it taste all right? I do have some honey."

"No, it's fine like it is," she lied. (It was all right to lie about small things.) "I keep getting the feeling that you were expecting me, Henry," she said, putting down her mug. "Were you? I came to talk about Jenine's letter. I assume you've received it."

Henry was sitting cross-legged on the bare floor across from her. He nodded. "I did have a feeling you'd come," he said, "Jenine mentioned in a postscript that she had talked to you."

How the letter was connected to his knowing she would come wasn't clear, though apparently it was to him. She herself hadn't known for certain she was coming until this morning, having spent much of the past three days alternating between thinking yes it would clarify things to see Henry and no, that it would do the opposite.

She didn't pursue it. "So what do you make of those men questioning her, Henry, what has been your reaction?" she asked.

He had been thinking about this all morning, ever since the mailman had delivered Jenine's letter. The news hadn't particularly surprised him; from the beginning he had assumed his protest would involve some kind of surveillance. Why the military should suddenly be questioning Jenine about his whereabouts on the 4th of July, though, he wasn't sure. He was inclined to think it was simply bureaucratic bungling, that the government took its time with small fry like himself and were only now getting around to doing their routine security check. But it could also be part of a heightened security alert involving some incident at the labs—a case of suspected espionage, for example, or a leak of some kind. "Maybe they suspect Walter of giving me secrets to pass to the Russians, who knows?" he added with a smile. "How is he lately, by the way, has he seemed especially up tight about anything?"

"Do you not see him, Henry, when he goes through the gates in the morning?" she asked.

"Yes, but he never speaks."

"Never?"

Henry shook his head.

"That's sad," Elizabeth said, and unaccountably felt tears come to her eyes. She blinked, and shifted her position in the uncomfortable chair. "To answer your question, no, I haven't noticed anything unusual in Walter, though I've been watching for something ever since Jenine called. I even fed him some mildly leading questions, but there was no reaction. He seems his usual unruffled self."

Henry looked thoughtful. "There could be something going on that he hasn't been told about, but it's most likely just the bureaucracy taking its own sweet time checking me out. I wouldn't worry about it, Elizabeth. Though it's possible it's a warning, a message of some kind, just to let me know they know I'm here. I'm sure they counted on Jenine passing it on." He grinned. "The optimistic view of all this is that their "warning" is evidence that I'm finally making some headway rattling some consciences over there, that someone is taking me seriously behind the gates of Edgewood Arsenal."

"That's your definition of optimism, is it?" she asked sharply, "that as soon as you start getting through to a few employees the government starts tailing you?"

He regarded her levelly. "Why not give it a positive spin, Elizabeth? Let's take the worst-case scenario: suppose the government had hard evidence of a terrorist plot against the labs at Edgewood or Detrick. If the plot succeeded, thousands could die, including, most likely, ourselves. Heightened security, on the other hand, might foil it, but at the cost of harmless people like myself getting dragged into the net of government surveillance. Which would you rather?"

Elizabeth grimaced. "OK, I've stacked the deck," Henry went on. "I don't mean to play the devil's advocate, but in the absence of evidence, I see no more warrant for pessimism than optimism, unless you prefer melodrama. If it makes me feel better to assume I'm being watched because my 'witnessing' is beginning to amount to something, why not? At least until the government gives me more information to think with. What else can we do? We don't know why these men were questioning Jenine about my whereabouts on the fourth of July, and the odds are we never will. Let's face it, this is a government of secrets, at least where military security is concerned; freedom of information stops at those gates, along with a few other rights one thought guaranteed by the Constitution."

He took a swallow of tea. "What's frustrating is that it seems a vicious circle. Given the nature of the things they make over there, such secrecy may be necessary; I wish it weren't so, but in the meantime government surveillance—and the fear and loss of privacy that that entails—is part of the price we pay for keeping these weapons 'secure.' It's something we have to live with, as long as we maintain genocidal arsenals."

"Jenine was worried that knowing you were under surveillance might make you paranoid," Elizabeth said.

Henry stretched his legs, then resumed his cross-legged position. "She's right, in a way, it does," he said. "But I didn't come into this expecting anything else. The U.S. government has the power to do whatever it thinks necessary to protect itself. The only limitation is they have to persuade the courts that their actions are in the service of "National Security." As far as I know, no court has ever refused them, which allows them to pretty much get away with anything. Now, it would be nice if they didn't see me as a threat to their security when I'm not, but if they choose to define me that way, there isn't much I can do about it. Actually, if surveillance is the worst thing they do to me, I shall consider myself lucky." He grinned. "Besides, it may be unnerving, but a little paranoia never hurt anyone. It keeps you on your toes."

Elizabeth took a sip of her tea, then carefully set the mug down. Her hand was shaking, she noticed; she feared her voice would too. "I also came to return your diary," she said, reaching into her bag. "I wanted to thank, you, Henry, for showing it to me. I didn't find it at all boring, though it was 'mostly politics,' as you said." She hesitated, giving him an opening, but when he didn't respond, said the first thing that came into her mind. "You know that poem by Blake in the beginning of the notebook, the one called "The Clod and the Pebble"? I wonder, have you ever thought of it in terms of yourself and your brother?"

The question was unexpected. As always, he took his time answering, carefully choosing his words. "Oddly enough, no, I haven't," he said finally. "I suppose it applies, but I don't like to think of Walter in terms of stone. "Or myself, for that matter," he added with a wry smile, "as a mindless clod of clay."

"How do you see your brother, Henry?"

She noticed that the question made him stiffen slightly. "That isn't easy to answer, Elizabeth," he said slowly, "mostly, I think, because I can see so many different Walters, at different times in his life. Like all of us, he changes as he takes on different roles. I don't much like what he is right now, but I still love what he was, and what he maybe will be at some point. He was a pretty good older brother, you know, up till the time I was twelve or so. He liked to teach me things. He had very inventive hands for making shadow images and string games, things like that. And marbles. He was very good at marbles."

"How was he when he lost?" Elizabeth asked with a smile.

Henry shrugged. "Like most of us at that age he didn't take it very well. Fortunately he didn't lose very often."

"What happened, then, that he stopped being such a good brother?"

Henry frowned. "I've thought about that," he said. "The obvious thing is my sister Sylvie's death; all of us seemed to change around that time. Walter reacted by drawing away, into himself. He started spending a lot of time alone, either at the gym or studying at the library, as if he all of a sudden thought the most important thing in life was to get top grades in order to get in to the top universities. He stopped having time for me, or for any of us."

He paused, offering her more tea, which she refused. "I guess by then I had changed a lot too. Didn't want anyone telling me what to do or what to learn, sort of like Stephen is right now, or that's how I see him. I guess I felt as if the whole adult world failed after Sylvie died. My father was angry, my mother pretty seriously depressed. The only thing that kept her in life, I think, was having to raise Jenine, and that seemed to take up what energy she had."

Elizabeth glanced at him. "So Jenine was in effect your little sister, from the time you were twelve? I guess I sort of knew that," she added, "but I never really thought about it. You must have helped raise her then."

"A bit, but not as much as you'd maybe think. Mom kept pretty tight watch on her. I don't remember being allowed to change her or anything when she was a baby, though I do remember reading her stories at night when she was two or three. *Goodnight, Moon:* she really liked *Goodnight, Moon.*"

Elizabeth smiled. "So did Stephen," she said. "How old were you, Henry, when you left home?"

"Seventeen: Jenine was just five. I didn't see much of the rest of her growing up."

"You left to join the commune, right? You were involved in the anti-war movement then."

"No, not right then; I wasted everybody's time and money for two years at Peabody first, studying piano. I started going to demonstrations during my first year, but not full-time. I was nineteen when I joined the commune."

Elizabeth looked away, at the small window set high up by the ceiling. Dust motes danced in the beam of light streaming through the parted curtains. "So one brother becomes a rebel and the other an over-achiever," she mused, "all because of a drunk driver."

Henry smiled. "Well, one could mention a few other determinants—genetics, to start with. And history: that always enters in. The Vietnam war, in my case. But why do you call Walter an "over-achiever?"

"Lord, Henry, I should think you'd know why better than anyone," she answered tartly. "He's so thoroughly single-minded he's unbalanced."

"No more so than I," Henry responded.

She didn't want to argue. Being an over-achiever or single-minded was the least of Walter's imbalances, and it didn't feel right to be talking any further about Walter; it felt disloyal. They sat in silence for a while, then Elizabeth took a deep breath and without prologue blurted out what she had come to say. "I'm going to leave Walter, Henry. I don't think I can live with him any more. The marriage isn't working."

Henry's eyes widened but he made no move, waiting for her to explain.

"I don't think we should live together any more," Elizabeth went on, "I don't love him, and I don't know now whether I ever did: I may have only been pretending, making the best of a bad situation. The marriage isn't good for me, it's fraudulent, I've finally come to admit that, and if it's not good for me, I don't see how it can be good for Walter. I don't think he'd want to live with me if he knew what I really feel; and I don't think I can go on pretending to feelings I don't have, and lying about those I do. I guess that's what I've come to realize the past few days. I've known all along the marriage wasn't good, I've just been pretending it was, for the children's sake, and Walter's too, I suppose. But it doesn't work that way, does it? It isn't good for children to get a picture of a pretend marriage as a model, is it? And how can I be anything other than a pretend parent if I'm a pretend wife?" She stopped in embarrassment, thinking she must sound hysterical. "I'm sorry if I've shocked you; I guess what I'm trying to say is that I think I have a real self inside, a self I remember from before I got pregnant with Philip. I don't think it's age, or motherhood, that has made me lose that person, I think it's been living with Walter and conforming to what he expects of me. Conforming to what this goddamn government expects of me as the wife of a servant of the military, which is what it amounts to. I know a separation will be hard for the children, but staying the way we are is surely just as bad, maybe even worse."

"I assume you've talked this through with Walter," Henry asked when she stopped. "You have considered marriage counselors, or some other kind of professional help?"

Elizabeth blushed. "No," she said wearily, "I haven't. I don't see any point to it. Walter would never consider any kind of therapy; he has nothing but scorn for psychology. And I haven't talked to him about my feelings because all this is still so new to me I haven't dared. I have to be clear in my own mind first, and there are still a lot of things I have to work out."

"So you haven't made any specific plans, or decided what you are going to do?"

"No," she replied, "no plan. I don't know when, exactly, I'll leave; it's just that I'm sure now I will."

He studied her for a moment, not her face but the slope of her shoulder. She had lowered her eyes and her face was obscured by her hair. He felt a wave of pity, as he would for a lost child. "Is there some way I can help you, Elizabeth?" he asked gently.

There was compassion in his voice, but she could detect nothing more, nothing that any man might not feel for a sister-in-law in distress. How could he help her? By *telling me you love me*, she wanted to cry, *telling me I can come stay with you and learn what it means to live according to principle. So I can learn to be you, Henry, because I think I love you....*

But she didn't say these things. Such dialogue occurred in films that ended with swelling music and a melting embrace, films with no day after where the lovers woke up to discover that the hero's commitment to his life's work—which is what the heroine loves in him—has been killed. All very well for Lancelot and Guinevere to become lovers, but what happened to the search for the Grail? In the real world the future existed; and she could see no way that a life with Henry could ever be put together, even if Walter and the children should vanish in a puff of smoke. A love affair with him would be a disaster:, for even if she succeeded in seducing him, he would hate himself for betraying his brother. He would never be able to disentangle his motives, and she would never be able to escape seeing herself as a pawn in a fraternal war. There was a reason why cultures all over the world forbade incest: what family could live day to day with such complications?

But knowing she must leave, that she must lie to him, made her want to cry. Because she could have loved him. She did love him.

It took effort, but somehow she mustered a smile. "Thank you, Henry, but you can't help me," she said. "I just wanted you to know what was going on between Walter and me. And to thank you for letting me know you a bit, through your diary."

He looked at her, puzzled, as if sensing that something important had just happened without knowing exactly what. "You're sincerely welcome," he said, "I appreciate your having read it."

She gathered her purse and pushed back her chair, all at once in haste to go. Henry rose and followed. "This won't be the last time I'll be seeing you, I trust?" he asked as they approached the door.

"No, of course not. I'm planning to take the boys to Baltimore for a while to see my sister, and then stay at my mother's for a few weeks, as soon as they finish camp. I'll consider what to do then."

"Walter isn't going to Ontario with you?"

"No," she said, "he'll be working. I won't tell him my plans until I get back. He's aware something is wrong, but he doesn't know I intend to leave him. Like I said, I have to work it out."

"Then it's good-bye only for now," he said, and held out his hand. She squeezed it and turned to leave, but then she couldn't help it, she drew him to her and brushed his lips with her own. Later she found it hard to believe that the ecstasy that shuddered through her hadn't been felt also by him, so much so that when he drew back, her first sensation was shock, followed by confusion. "Good luck to you, Henry," she whispered, "keep in touch," and moved away, stepping outside quickly, before she could give in to further temptation. The door closed behind her.

She sat in the car for a minute staring at the ignition key, tears crowding her throat. There was no point in going back, she told herself. It was finished, over. She started the car, wondering if what she had just done was an example of free will. If so, she should be feeling proud of herself; she should be applauding her virtue, cheering the triumph of reason. She had gone to the cliff and prudently stepped back, saving herself and her family who knows how much grief. Why then did it taste so bitter? Or is that what "maturity" tasted like?"

She drove herself back feeling like a prison guard transporting an inmate to prison. Two blocks from her house she stopped at a 7-11 and went in and bought a pack of cigarettes. As a further act of free will, she would give up giving them up.

CHAPTER 10

▼

After driving to Pennsylvania and collecting the boys from camp, they spent three civil days at home before she and Stephen and Philip were to leave for Baltimore. During that time Elizabeth slept on the couch. When Stephen came down early one morning and found her there, she told him the noise of the air conditioner in the bedroom bothered her.

Her plan was to take the bus to Baltimore and a cab to her sister's, stay there for the weekend and then catch the plane to Toronto, where she would rent a car and drive the rest of the way to her mother's. Ordinarily she didn't like to drive such distances by herself, but the 401, linking Toronto and Montreal, was a familiar road. She would at least have no worries about getting lost.

Walter drove them to the bus station and transferred their luggage to the bus. He hugged the boys and admonished them, unnecessarily, Elizabeth thought, to "be on their best behavior." She said good-bye and promised to call as soon as they were settled. He gave her a perfunctory kiss, which she allowed, trying not to wonder if it was their last.

At her sister's she kept up the part of the cheerful mom taking the children to visit their grandmother, with a stop en route to see their Aunt Linda and Uncle Daniel. The children, who didn't particularly care for either aunt or uncle, weren't as good at keeping up pretenses. Elizabeth couldn't blame them; she herself kept comparing this brother-in-law to Henry, weighing him in the balance and finding him wanting. The two men could hardly have been more different. She disliked Daniel's too conventional handsomeness. He was too conventionally everything, in her judgment, one of those people who prided themselves on not being "showy" about wealth while living in tasteful luxury. Among other things, she disliked the way he fancied himself a connoisseur of wine. Since she herself could taste no difference between the medium-priced and the high-priced, it seemed to her an affectation. Daniel was too smooth, too poised, and too patronizing. When she first met him she had thought of him as the perfect Ken doll to her sister's Barbie. She still saw him that way, only now he was a more polished, grown-up version. The only thing Elizabeth liked polished was semi-precious stones.

At least Walter wasn't like that: he wasn't greedy for status, as long as his physical comfort was assured. He wasn't vain of his appearance either, she reflected, although maybe he was becoming so, what with this new exercise machine. It occurred to her to wonder if he was unconsciously grooming himself for the possibility of waking up single one day, as if on some level he was preparing for her to leave....

She dismissed the thought and tried to concentrate. They were sitting around Linda's elaborate dinner table, where the room was sparkling with several dozen candles. She had to admit they were beautiful, their tiny flares of light echoing in the polished mahogany table, but she couldn't help thinking of the maid that had to accompany all this: whoever was polishing this table and cleaning a hundred candle holders wasn't Linda. And where on earth did they store this many candles, or did they just throw them away after the evening's use? Either way, it seemed extravagant; intended to flatter, to honor the guests, it was making at least one of them, her, uncomfortable instead. The children, she noticed, were awed, particularly when a maid in a hairnet and apron came in with the entree, in this case a tureen of beef bourguignonne. "It's just like in a restaurant," Stephen whispered as she served him. Unfortunately, Linda heard him. "Not at all, Stephen," she said reprovingly, "it's just a special occasion for family."

A silence fell, lasting until the maid had finished serving and retreated behind the swinging doors. "You look like you're concentrating on something, Elizabeth," Linda said when the silence persisted. "Whatever are you thinking?"

"I'm sure she's concentrating on this delicious beef," Daniel put in, with practiced gallantry.

"Actually, I was thinking about Virginia Woolf's *To The Lighthouse*," Elizabeth replied. "Have either of you read it? There's a lovely scene where the main character, Mrs. Ramsay, serves beef bourguignonne."

"Sorry, I haven't," her sister returned. "She served it herself, I take it?"

"I wasn't implying any criticism, Linda, it's just that as soon as I smelled the beef bourguignonne I happened to think of its description in the novel."

"Wasn't Virginia Woolf a lesbian?" Daniel inquired.

Elizabeth bridled. "She was primarily a writer," she said. "I don't see how who she was sleeping with is relevant."

"You don't believe there is such a thing as the lesbian sensibility then?"

There was nothing but curiosity in his tone, but Elizabeth felt baited. "No," she said shortly.

"Oh you two," Linda interrupted. "You're already at it."

From their first meeting, Elizabeth and Daniel had disliked each other, within minutes of their introduction getting into a passionate argument, about the writer, Ayn Rand, of all things. Linda preferred to believe that the differences between them were purely political, but to Elizabeth that seemed a shallow analysis; beneath the politics was a radical clash of values and temperaments. Fortunately Linda was mostly unaware of how strong their mutual dislike was, though she instinctively contrived to keep them apart as much as possible. During the time Elizabeth was there, Daniel conveniently spent most of his time elsewhere, presumably at the hospital.

The next morning, a Saturday, she and Linda went shopping, after which they took the children to the zoo. The next day Philip begged to go out to Pimlico to "watch the horses," which his aunt predictably vetoed. There would be horses enough in Ontario, she said, there would be bunches of them standing in the shade all along the road to his grandmother's.

Horses standing still didn't interest Philip; he wanted to see them raced, surrounded by the excitement of betting. The compromise was a mall that had a small video arcade, followed by pizza at an expensive Italian restaurant.

Back at home they made an attempt at playing charades (Linda's idea), but it didn't go very well. The four of them weren't familiar with the same books or films, which made guessing the titles too difficult. Linda eventually gave up and went to bed, mentioning a headache, though when Elizabeth later passed her room she could hear the television on. She allowed the boys to cajole her into a game of pinochle, after which she sent them to their room to get their pajamas on, reminding them they had to be at the airport at ten.

*   *   *   *

The flight went smoothly, the only mishap Stephen's knocking over his ginger ale. She had no trouble renting a car at the airport. The traffic leaving Toronto, however, was unnerving. It had been three years since she had done this, three years of living in a small town where she mostly walked wherever she wanted to go (unless it was to the mall for something heavy, like groceries), a place with two-lane roads where cars moved at a reasonable speed. The vehicles whizzing past her from so many directions, particularly huge tanker trucks passing her as if she was standing still, was dizzying.

It was better once they got away from Toronto and the six lanes went down to four. To distract herself she turned the radio on, playing with the dial until she found the CBC, knowing instantly when she had by its tenor and tone. The intelligent-sounding voices filled her with delight, like voices of old friends she had missed without knowing it. She had grown up with the CBC; the dial had been set there on every radio in her mother's house.

Just outside Port Hope they stopped for sandwiches and milkshakes. "Onion rings or French fries but not both," she told the boys as they waited in line, concerned that too much fried food would lead to car-sickness, which Stephen in particular was prone to. After some argument, French fries won. Elizabeth drank her coffee, envying the boys their milkshakes, annoyed by their straw-slurping. She was convinced they did it on purpose to irritate her, to "get her goat," as her mother would say. To prove that they hadn't, she said nothing.

She paid with American money, marveling at how much change she received. They set off. The signs to familiar-sounding towns drifted by, Cobourg, Trenton, Belleville, Kingston. At Brockville, they turned north.

"How much longer mom?" Philip asked for the fifth time.

"About thirty minutes," she said. "Look, there are the horses your Aunt Linda was talking about." She slowed the car, pointing to a field where five horses, including a colt, were standing in the shade of a tree. Stephen watched them longingly through the window.

"All they're doing is switching their tails," Philip complained.

"They're keeping flies off each other, they cooperate that way," Stephen said.

"And aren't they beautiful," Elizabeth said.

Her back was stiff and her eyes were smarting when they pulled into the driveway, after an interminable ten minutes of jouncing around on the winding unpaved road to her mother's cottage. Once out of the car she glimpsed through the trees the wide expanse of Lake Channing glittering in the sun, and her fatigue lifted. Without unpacking, leaving the car as it was, she took the path down to the dock. She wouldn't stay long, she told herself, she needed to go to the bathroom and her mother would consider her behavior rude, but her eyes were clamoring for an uncluttered view of the flat expanse of water, her ears for the sound of it against the shore.

Happiness rippled through her the minute her feet touched the worn gray boards of the dock. She took off her sandals, flushed with gratitude that this place was still here, the air so clear, so exhilarating to breathe. She stood on tiptoe and stretched her arms as far as they would go, thanking the sky, the forested shore, the puffy white clouds. A native saying she had read somewhere, *"Beauty is all around you,"* came back to her: she shivered, remembering it. She was home. Free. For two whole weeks, even longer if she chose, she could come out here on this dock and commune with the view whenever she wished. She would have to spend time with her mother, of course, and time, a good deal of it, with Philip and Stephen—the lake was too deep and their swimming and canoeing skills too undeveloped to let them go off by themselves, particularly when the waves were choppy. But still there would be time to be out here, alone, in delicious solitude, where she somehow had to reach a decision about what she wanted to do, what her feelings for Henry were, what she should do about her marriage, maybe writing in that notebook she bought a week ago and not yet opened. She had brought it with her, stuffing it in her suitcase at the last moment.

But first she must greet her mother, rescue her, if need be, from her wound-up grandsons, focus their energy by setting them to help her unpack the car and finding their bathing suits. She treated her eyes to one last vision of the lake, and climbed back up the path.

✳   ✳   ✳   ✳

Esther Crawford was sitting on the porch in her rocking chair when her daughter opened the screen door. She put aside the bowl of peas she was shelling and stood up to greet her.

"Hi, mom," Elizabeth said after they hugged. "Sorry, I didn't come in right away, I felt like stretching my legs so I went straight down to the lake."

"I know, I figured that's where you were," Esther said placidly, "It's fine, sit down, sit down." She motioned Elizabeth to a lawn chair and sat down herself, picking up the bowl of peas. Her daughter was looking well, she thought, healthy, tanned. She had the right feel about her too, when they embraced: no flab, but good solid flesh on her bones. She was wearing white slacks and a lavender singlet. It was a flattering color.

Elizabeth crossed to the kitchen door and peered inside. "Where are the boys?" she asked.

"In the bedroom, trying to coax the cat from under the bed."

"Ah, Lotus—how is she?" Her mother's cat, a Siamese, was fifteen years old.

"Getting on in years, like me, but still getting around well enough," Esther replied.

Her mother was sixty-eight, not all that old these days, and she looked even younger than that, at least when she was sitting down; her once-blonde, now mouse-brown hair hadn't turned gray yet, except a touch about the temples. When she stood up and moved about, though, stiffly, she looked years older.

"How is the arthritis, mum, are you taking anything for it?"

Esther smiled. "Chamomile tea," she said. "Home-grown: I've got a pot of it in the kitchen. You want some?"

She moved to get up but Elizabeth stopped her. "Sit still, mum, I'll get it," she said, "I want to check on the boys."

Esther sat back in the rocker, relieved that Elizabeth was here to take care of things. She set the bowl of peas on the floor and folded her hands in her lap, enjoying the rippling sound the small waves were making as they touched the shore. She didn't come out to the cottage much any more; it was more comfortable in her apartment in Brockville, where she had her friends. She came out here two days ago, and what with cleaning up the remains of wildlife (mice droppings, mostly) and sweeping out a year's worth of dust, she hadn't had much time to sit still.

The cleaning had been tiring, but children needed a clean environment. It was bad enough you had to cope with dirt and the things it bred when you were outside, you didn't need to have it inside too. Not that her grandsons would appreciate how clean the cottage was, she thought, any more than she had appreciated her own clean house when she was a child, but you picked such things up whether you were aware of them or not. When you polished wooden furniture it gleamed and reflected light, it was beautiful, and somehow you absorbed the beauty, as if through your skin. Esther believed quite firmly that growing up in aesthetically pleasing surroundings nurtured character.

She rocked slowly in the chair, allowing herself to bask for a moment in the day's accomplishments. Everything was in order, roast and potatoes and carrots in the oven, lemon cake and brownies baked fresh this morning. Dinner would be at six o'clock, just as she had planned.

It was important to do things on time, she believed, important to complete the tasks you set yourself. Otherwise, living alone, you tended to drift and became detached. Too much unstructured time wasn't good, you had to hold it in check with rituals and chores. This was something the old shared with the young, she thought, a need for structured time, though it was good for people at any age.

She wondered what the boys were doing. From the glimpse she had had of them, they seemed well too, though Stephen was maybe a bit pale. He looked rumpled, as if he had been sleeping in the car. They had waved hello as they came up the porch steps, stopping long enough to give her a hug and then scampering off to the bathroom. The next thing she knew they were chasing the cat. They seemed to have quieted down now, which must mean they were watching television. Already, she thought with a sigh.

She had moved the television set to Elizabeth's bedroom the night before, hoping it would be used sparingly, and mostly as a rainy-day anti-boredom device. It had surprised her that the old thing still worked. All you could get on it was the CBC from Kingston and CBS from New York, but this could be a good thing, hopefully cutting down the amount of time Stephen and Philip would spend watching it. She wondered how she'd last the visit if the weather turned rainy. There were several games in the cupboard, Monopoly and Parchesi and dominoes and cards, but the cottage was tiny and she couldn't handle a lot of noise. Elizabeth would have to take the children to the village, to the video store, if they got bored. There wasn't much of a selection there either, but they would have to make do.

She had tested the VCR the night before, so she knew it was working. She'd borrowed *Modern Times* from the library and watched it. She no longer worked at the library, but everyone who did still knew her and let her keep books and video tapes for as long as she wanted. To her surprise, *Modern Times*, which she had seen years ago, was still funny. She thought Stephen and Philip might like it.

Elizabeth returned, bearing a tray with tea things. She poured herself a cup and settled back in the lounge chair. "The boys are watching cartoons," she said as she sat down. "I suspect it's an excuse to take a nap without admitting it. They've been traveling all day, they're tired. When is dinner, mum?"

Esther smiled. "At six, as always. It's all ready but the gravy, which doesn't need seeing to for half an hour yet. Are you too tired for a talk?"

"No, not at all, but I'd rather talk about you, if you don't mind. I suspect I'm too tired to think straight about myself."

Something in her tone aroused Esther's suspicion, as if a faint warning bell had sounded, but she didn't pursue it. She found the remark mildly irritating. Her daughter wasn't the only one who was tired; she too would rather listen than talk. Conversation could be a burden sometimes, having to think up things to say. "Well, not much to tell about my life that you don't already know," she responded. "It doesn't change much. I go for walks, I read my library books. I play bridge and visit with friends. I tend my plants. I watch television."

"What do you usually watch, mum?"

"*Cheers* mostly, sometimes *Dallas*, if I'm really bored."

"Don't you watch the news any more?" Elizabeth asked.

"Not much, not on TV. I listen on the radio when I'm fixing dinner. Occasionally I look at *The National* and *The Journal*, if I'm not too tired. Watching that late though, I don't pay much attention, except when something really awful happens, like with Chernobyl. I watched the news a lot then; for that whole week I hardly went outside, and I didn't drink any milk either. Lord knows what those cows picked up, even over here, that fall-out went all over. But you know that, we talked about it on the phone, remember? Did you make the boys stop drinking milk, by the way, like I suggested?"

Elizabeth frowned, feeling guilty, for no, she hadn't. She had tried, but it had precipitated a row, particularly with Stephen. Moreover, she knew that even if she succeeded in banning milk there would be an even bigger fight over cheese, which was a staple of everyone's diet, including her own; and since cheese came from milk, what was the point? "They didn't drink much milk in April, but we did eat cheese," she said apologetically. "Walter pooh-poohed the idea that it was dangerous, and I'm afraid I capitulated."

"Well, at least you tried," Esther said consolingly.

The remark intensified Elizabeth's discomfort. She hadn't tried, not really; looking back on it, her gestures in that direction were pitiful. Not that anyone else's was much different. A nuclear disaster happens, and instead of demanding that governments all over the world shut down or phase out such horrors, everyone responded by being cautious about the amount of milk they let their children drink. It was selfish, frighteningly so. What about the children in the Ukraine?

She wondered if Henry was influencing her thinking, as if he had made her more sensitive to the ethical dimension of things, more aware of selfishness. But she couldn't explain that to her mother, and changed the subject.

"Do you remember, mum, when you first bought this place? Daddy was still alive then. He was pretty good out here, about drinking, I mean, as if this was a healing place for him. We had some good times on this lake, didn't we? It was the best thing you ever bought."

"Well, it will belong to you and the boys when I go," Esther said. She knew that wasn't what Elizabeth had meant, but she didn't want to talk about Elizabeth's father. Yes, there had been good times out here but also not so good times that she didn't want to remember. She stood up. "I better see to these peas, or they won't be ready when the rest is. Come on in and set the table for me and get your children awake. Nothing worse than a good dinner spoiled by grumpy children."

Elizabeth sighed, then smiled. Her mother was right. Few things were worse.

*   *   *   *

After the dishes and an interminable game of Monopoly with the boys, she was more than ready for bed. She lay for a long while in the tub, making plans for the next few days, a mental list of what needed sorting out, primarily what she owed to herself and what she owed the children, whether they would be worse off with a single mother or an unhappily married one, one who, for all she knew, might be even unhappier single, and definitely poorer. Until she was firm in her mind about all that, she should do her best to put Henry completely from mind. If by the end of the week her feelings were still a muddle, she would have a long talk with her mother and ask her advice.

Unfortunately, her plan was never put into practice. When she was making her bed the next morning, her mother had a call from a close friend, Mary Winston, whose husband had just had a stroke. Mary was semi-hysterical, but Esther gathered that the husband was in the hospital at the moment, mute and paralyzed on one side; the doctors didn't know yet if it was temporary. Esther felt she had to go back to town for a few days to give Mary moral support. She would come back when she could, she said.

It was hot and cloudless and still. After her mother left, Elizabeth loaded up the picnic basket and took the boys to their favorite place, Deer Island, which was twenty-minutes by canoe from their dock. She steered from the back, with Stephen in the middle and Philip in front. He was getting pretty good at paddling, she noticed. She wondered if she should let him take over the steering on the way home, but then Stephen would insist on being up front (it was his turn, after all), and with the two of them navigating, it might take hours to get home. Not today, she thought, maybe later in the summer, after Philip had more practice.

They beached the canoe and clambered out onto the island. The boys raced each other to their favorite swimming spot. "No going in the water till I get there," Elizabeth yelled after them, but she didn't rush to join them. Instead she ambled, noting the changes since she'd been here last. She stopped and briefly mourned her favorite birch, which used to crown the cliff across from the cove; it had been blown over in a storm, and now lay in jagged fragments on the granite shelf. The blueberry bushes along the rocks, which the birds had already picked over, looked scruffy, their leaves more red than green. Everything was in need of rain; even the large patches of moss at the far end of the island, ordinarily at this time of year a lush deep green, were bleached to a pale yellow.

She spread the picnic blanket in their accustomed place beside an old jack pine, the only spot offering shade close to the water. She settled her back against the trunk and unpacked the rest of the basket: the plastic box holding their sandwiches, juice, water, a small thermos of coffee, a paperback copy of Margaret Lawrence's *The Stone Angel* which she had found on her mother's bookshelf. At the bottom, her lighter and pack of Benson & Hedges; and her new spiral notebook and pen.

She picked up *The Stone Angel* and started to read. The boys had been swimming and diving off the rocks, but now they began performing mock "water ballet" routines, competing for her attention. She watched and applauded till they finally tired of it and went off to play games in the small patch of woods in the island's center. She put her book aside and picked up her notebook.

July 29, 1986, she wrote at the top of the page, much as if she were writing a letter. Well, she was, she reflected, a letter to herself. The problem was she didn't know how to begin.

Begin with the sorrow, she wrote in shorthand, as if a voice not her own was speaking through her pen. *Write of the pain just now at seeing Philip and Stephen so happy out here, when what you see and they don't is how fragile that happiness is. They seem so oblivious to any problems in their parents' marriage, they don't know yet how things beyond their control can suddenly change their lives....*

She stopped, considering. That might be true of Philip, but it wasn't necessarily true of Stephen. She had caught him looking at her in an odd way one night at the dinner table at home, as if he had picked up on something in her tone, or Walter's, that had made him suddenly afraid. She was sure she hadn't imagined it. He had looked so vulnerable, suddenly, and anguished.

She put down her pen and reached in the pocket of her beach robe for a tissue. It wouldn't do, this writing business; it only brought on tears. She didn't want the boys to come back and find her crying, not when she couldn't answer the questions they would surely ask. Chin up, she said to herself, which is what her father used to say when she started crying about something. "Chin up, here's looking at you, kid," in his best Humphrey Bogart voice.

She put the notebook and pen back in the basket. The heat had grown in intensity. It was time for a swim. She took off her sandals and walked barefoot down to the granite boulder at the lake's edge that sloped gradually into the water. She sat down on it, testing the water with her toes. It was deliciously cool. Without further thought she slipped in.

A shiver of bodily ecstasy went through her the moment the water enveloped her shoulders, every nerve in her skin swooning with gratitude at its miraculous softness. She dived, came up for air, floated on her back. Her grief of a moment ago slid away, and she gave herself up to sensation, the crystalline blue of the sky, the warm pinks and mauves of the rocks, the silhouette of the jack pine, majestic in its gaunt, craggy beauty. The dilemmas of her life melted, Walter, the children, Henry's grave, lovable face. She swam a few strokes, keeping the sun at her back. "Why this is Heaven, nor am I out of it," she thought, the words drifting into her mind, not hers, but whose? Ah yes, Milton, but she had the quote wrong. What Milton had Satan say when he was with Eve in the garden, before the Fall, was "*Why this is Hell, nor am I out of it.*" She'd rewritten it.

Again she dove beneath the water and came up. She had always believed there was no purer water in the world than this spring-fed lake. Many people fished here, but they used motor boats sparingly, and it was enormously deep, not here in this cove where they swam, but in the center of the lake, where it was a hundred feet or more, deep enough to swallow whole horses and sleighs in the old days when they drove out in March and the ice had thawed earlier than they expected. She'd read a history of this lake once, years ago. The granite rocks were part of the Canadian shield, presumably the oldest rocks on earth, existing from the beginning, when the planet first formed. The lake, and her mother's cottage, had been Algonquin land till 1816, when George IV rewarded a British Colonel named Landsdowne for his service in the Napoleonic wars by giving him 2,000 acres in "Terra Nullus," as Ontario was called, specified in British maps as "Unoccupied Land in His Majesty's Dominions." Apparently the King just rolled out a map of this land, a place neither of them had ever seen, and asked the Colonel where he wanted his ten thousand acres. He pointed to this lake and the land around it. The Indians weren't told, of course, nor did the book she'd read say where they went, only that they had "moved on."

As she climbed out and dried herself, she could hear the boys laughing and shouting to each other in the woods. She followed the path through the trees to where they were, and summoned them back to the blanket. After they ate, they skipped stones for a while, something Walter had taught them; she remembered his saying to her once that he had learned it from Sylvie. The boys' skill was far superior to her own. Stephen finally won with a stone that skipped seven times.

On the trip home she sat in the middle and let the two of them paddle, Philip steering from the back, Stephen in the front. Their course was a bit zigzag, but not as bad as she expected.

After dinner that night the telephone rang again. This time it was Walter, with even more shocking news. Henry was dead. Someone had shot him, just outside the gates of the lab.

Mechanically she hung up the phone, then dialed Air Canada to change their tickets. She called her mother in Brockville and explained what was happening. The next morning she closed up the cottage and drove to Toronto. Within an hour they were in the air, and a few hours later at the Baltimore Airport, where Walter met them. Henry's funeral was the following day, in Abbottsford.

CHAPTER 11

▼

January 2, 1991

One of my New Year's resolutions last night was to take up writing in this notebook again. Through practice, I may get the hang of it, but at the moment it feels stilted and cramped. I don't see anything in my life worth recording: I am a divorced mother of two, or maybe I should say of one and a half, since I see Philip for less than half the year, and this will shrink even more when he's in university. He has just turned seventeen, and his roots are in Maryland, where his friends and his father's family are. He's an American.

I feel that I've lost Philip. More and more he seems completely his father's son, and maybe always was. I try to accept our estrangement as being a matter of temperament, or the good old generation gap, but I suspect it's deeper than that. I'm not sure he trusts me, or anyone for that matter. He certainly doesn't trust me with his inner life; for all I know he doesn't have one. If only he were interested in something other than technology and computer games; he's become such a smart-ass, a techno-know-it-all. Most of the time we don't have much to say to each other, particularly on the phone. When he's here, he chafes (my house doesn't have enough electronic gizmos to suit him) and ends up annoying me because of his subtle bullying of Stephen. It makes me feel guilty to harbor such negative feelings about him, but there they are.

Why did I make this New Year's resolution in the first place? I was visiting a friend in Toronto over the holiday, Cindy from way back in my U. of T. days. She had surprised me by calling last month and inviting me to come. I was dubious about going—travel during the holidays, by train, bus or car, can be a nightmare up here—but I went; and I enjoyed myself.

Cindy still seems happy with Jeff after being together for seven years, and she's making a go of her photo business. The only cloud is that they've been trying for over two years to conceive and haven't been able to. She doesn't want to go the route of fertility treatments, she said, unless it was absolutely necessary. She claimed to be still hopeful, but that could have been holiday cheer.

I liked Jeff. His job is some complicated kind of computer mapping for various local governments, about which I know nothing and couldn't care less, but he seemed intelligent and very affectionate with Cindy. He also has a good sense of humor, which somewhat makes up for his pot belly. Maybe not his hairiness, though, which I presume extends to both his back and chest: in other words, physically not my type.

There was a man there, though, who was—an Indian named Raj Singh who looked like he could have been a Bollywood film star if his parents had stayed in Calcutta: beautiful nose, smooth bronze skin, deep brown eyes with thick black lashes. Unfortunately, his wife, who was in the kitchen when I first started talking to him, turned out to be as beautiful as he, with a Ph.D. to match. She was dressed in one of those ravishing saris, this one shimmering with silvers and violets and blues. Actually, both of them were fun to talk to; we had a lively conversation about Bergman's films, of all things. They had even seen Shame, and agreed with me that it was one of his most powerful.

It may have been the combination of grass and champagne, but I was feeling unusually buoyant that night. When someone put "You Can't Always Get What You Want" on the stereo, I went off on a long thought-train about the way the essence of Time is its Constant Vanishing, and that writing was a way to hold it back for a while, like building a sea wall to keep it at bay. In reality it's probably more like a sand castle, but I made a resolution to write, at least two or three times during the year.

But it feels like I'm talking to myself, which as everyone knows is a sign of dottiness.

August 1

I only found this notebook the day before yesterday, when I was looking through the jumble drawer at home, which is why there's a six-month gap. I stuck it in my purse and brought it out to the cottage.

When I woke up this morning, there was a report on the news that two days ago there was a near-miss accident at the Nine Mile Island reactor in Oswego, New York, a nuclear power plant I'd never heard of, right across the river from Kingston. A power failure due to a thunderstorm blacked out the control room. The operators managed after several hours to shut it down, by flashlight; if they had failed, I would have had to flee. Kingston is only sixty miles from here, and the way the winds were blowing. this cottage and the homes of thousands of others would have been directly in the path of the radiation plume.

It's incredible that we should have to live under this kind of threat—we, meaning the human race. That a malfunctioning machine in somebody else's country could all of a sudden go haywire and spew radiation over my small corner of paradise—indeed, kill me and my children and thousands of my countrymen—is outrageous.

So too is our passivity. But what can anyone do? There is so much ignorance. Bush is as bad as Reagan on anything nuclear, and our own Prime Minister is no better.

It is a beautiful August day, warm and rustly. Rippling of water, sweep of wind. Sunlight on bright green leaves, new-washed by last night's rain. And some idiotic American nuclear reactor could take it all away?

I finally found a buyer for the Mannings' house this week and closed the deal. Together with the sale of the cottage on Deer Lake I feel entitled to a week's vacation out here by myself. The boys left yesterday for Maryland. They will spend the rest of the summer with Walter, who wanted to take them to California when he goes to a conference in Frisco. All told, it was a trying visit. Philip seems less and less to enjoy the natural world out here. For some reason, blood type or type of sweat or something, he seems to attract the few hateful insects we have, horse flies in particular, who have never bitten me or Stephen. After having been stung twice, he refused to go canoeing any more, and ventured out to swim only on days when it was seriously hot. Since there weren't many of those (it's been an unusually cool, wet summer), he was even antsier than usual. All he did was watch television and play that interminable Tetris game over and over, or worse, that other game he brought with him, "The Ancient Art of War." We got into an argument about that one, or rather I got myself steamed and started yelling about values and he ignored me.

It seems almost diabolical when the traits you most disliked in your son's father show up in your son. I wonder if Walter sees things he doesn't like about me in Stephen and feels the same way.

I will miss Stephen, but I admit to being elated at the prospect of having time alone to read, and maybe to write, now that I've found this notebook. All I've managed in the book department this summer was A. S. Byatt's Possession, a tour de force of Victorian scholarship that seemed at times endless. I put it down a third of the way through, asking myself why I should spend forty hours reading this intricate filigree about two poets who never lived. It reminds me of Coleridge's "Christabel" (as it is probably meant to do), a fairy fragment about a world that never was, a lost dwelling place for which we presumably yearn known as the "World of the Imagination." I don't believe it exists. Yet while I'm reading the novel, the character of Christabel LaMotte is as real for me as Emily Bronte, or any other writer.

August 20

The time I thought I would have to read seems to have been pre-empted by the extraordinary political drama going on, which has kept me far more tethered to the television than usual. Two days ago Gorbachev was overthrown, in a bizarre coup d'etat that isn't over yet. I feel like we're on a roller coaster, with today a day of hope—the people in the streets in Moscow rallying to support their mayor, Boris Yeltsin, while the tanks of the Soviet Army played cat and mouse. Gorbachev is still being held prisoner somewhere, but there are rumors that three of the eight conspirators, including the KGB head, have resigned. Also rumors that some army units have defected. The pundits tonight on the CBC dashed cold water on this, however, managing to convince me that the Yeltsin forces will most likely be crushed in a bloody massacre, a repeat of Tianamen Square.

In the midst of my gloom I was suddenly shaken by an appalling question: since no one knows who's in charge of the Soviet Union at the moment, who the hell is in charge of the missiles? What's the nuclear chain of command in a Russian civil war? We could be two steps from Armageddon if the conspirators get paranoid and think the U.S. might take advantage of their confusion to attack the country. They might even try a pre-emptive strike of their own, particularly if there's some technical glitch, like one of their computers malfunctioning and mistaking blips for incoming missiles. They are on a hair-trigger alert, after all, and if such a thing should happen, it's bye-bye planet, that's all she wrote, folks, the end of our nuclear Loony Tunes.

Not easy to sleep with such thoughts; I go back to A. S. Byatt.

August 21

Unbelievably, the military coup has been defeated. Gorbachev is back in power, together with Yeltsin. I have been doing little but listening to National Public Radio and watching both the CBC and CNN. The CBC is consistently more pessimistic.

Things are happening at such speed, newspapers are obsolete before you get to read them. In the Globe & Mail I bought this morning, the coup is still going on.

The conspirators have made fools of themselves; no one knows at the moment where they have fled. Their blind spot was to underestimate the Russian peoples' love for their newly-tasted freedom. The smartest thing Gorbachev ever did to protect himself was glasnost—*unleashing Russian historians to tell the truth about the Stalinist past.*

I am grateful enough to believe for a moment in God: what might have happened if it had gone the other way is too terrible to think about. The good guys have actually won one! Unless God is a joker, and the instability of democracy leads to yet another Stalin. But we've been given a reprieve.

On the radio, in Berlin, thousands of people were singing "We Shall Overcome." They are celebrating in all the Russian republics. "Freedom has won." What happens now? Does the Soviet Union dissolve? It is all happening too quickly.

What an astonishing three-day drama this has been, like a mini-series with a happy ending. The David vs. Goliath script, with David for a change winning. People Power winning.

Surely the photo image of the year will be the celebrating Russian crowds toppling that gigantic statue of the founder of the KGB. It looked like Gulliver being pulled down by the Lilliputians. The police stood by and watched, as did the KGB from their windows.

August 22

I woke up this morning to Gorbachev's press conference (the joke is that the press conference lasted longer than the coup)—how the plotters had come to him and cut his phones; how the palace guard had remained loyal, putting together a radio receiver that allowed them to reach the BBC and the Voice of America. (Ironically, it was Gorbachev who had stopped the practice of jamming these broadcasts). How he had made a tape that was smuggled out, telling the world that he wasn't ill, that the plot-ters were acting illegally.

My mind just keeps trilling, "amazing, amazing." What extraordinary euphoria accompanies a non-violent revolution! One young Russian was filmed saying, "From now on, we'll love each other." Well, that's not likely, but the Russians finally have something to be proud of, which they haven't had in a long time, not since the last rev-olution, in fact, before it turned horrible. This one was bloodless, a triumph of Gan-dhi's spirit—and perhaps the examples of Haiti and the Philippines. Imagine, one huge part of the world seems actually to have learned not to try to change their govern-ment by force or violence! It was the Russian Army that upheld democracy, obeying democracy's first principle—that armies must not be used as an instrument against their own people, that power seized by the bullet rather than the ballot is illegitimate power, and should not be obeyed.

On the second day of the coup, Yeltsin called for massive civil disobedience and a general strike. The latter didn't materialize, but the former did. One hundred Rus-sians poured into the square around the Russian Parliament and built barricades of steel beams and trolley cars. Inside, Yeltsin and other members of the parliament dis-tributed gas masks and made Molotov cocktails (imagine!). When one of the armored personnel carriers defected, Yeltsin climbed on top of it and made a speech, Russian flags waving in the background. Four civilians were killed when a renegade unit tried to crush the barricade, and the opposition wasn't entirely non-violent—Molotov cock-tails were thrown at the tanks, one of which caught fire—but on the whole it was miraculously peaceful.

What's the next act? The world has been spinning too fast since 1988. They should declare a moratorium on change until we all catch up.

The dark side is that the Russian economy is in shambles, with the near certainty of hyper-inflation, maybe even famine. There seems to be considerable anarchy every-where. Serbia is gobbling up Croatia, helping itself to large chunks of territory. The Middle East peace conference agreed to before Gorbachev's kidnapping is on hold. I feel very lucky to be living where I am.

I found the following in The New Yorker this week, which I picked up on my way to the dentist. It's by someone called Debora Greger, a modernized version of Arnold's "Dover Beach":

Air-Conditioned Air

It's late. The street light
lies fair upon the street, on the coast
of Florida it gleams. Sea turtles lay their eggs

in the parking lots of hotels,
glimmering and vast. Come to the window,
air-conditioned is the night air,

you can hear the comfort of its roar
begin to chill and then begin again
the flow of something human drowning the sea

somewhere far below our room.
The air is calm tonight, the same air
as tomorrow, and we are here.

Look how the little candelabra
of a pleasure boat is borne by the darkness
of water over the old slave route.

Sometimes I think the only kind of Americans I can abide are anti-American ones, those who remember what the sea sounded like before air-conditioners, who don't forget the "dark water over the old slave routes."

August 23

Russia's heady drama continues. Carla called from Kingston to share her amazement.

Tolstoy deserves as much credit for this revolution as Gandhi—he was, after all, one of Gandhi's teachers. I've always thought of Russia as the land of Great Souls, ever since my Russian literature course in university. At a time when we were supposed to hate and fear the Russians, I loved them—not Stalin and Kruschev and Breznev and the rest but the people who suffered, century after century, under the world's worst governments. Russia to me was Tolstoy, Dostoevsky, Chekov, not Lenin. It was Eisen-

stein and Prokofiev, Tchaikovsky, Mussorgsky, Stravinsky. I know better now, but I still romanticize the Russians.

Spent most of the morning with the papers, reading with horror an American wire service report offering a new explanation of why the Russian crowds pulled down the statue of the founder of the KGB. Apparently their real goal had been to storm Lenin's tomb and drag out his body; someone managed to redirect them to Drzynski's statue instead.

If this is true, all I can say is thank god for that Someone: I can't think of anything more inflammatory than the desecration of Lenin's corpse. The idea is revolting, ringing with overtones of Freud's primal horde cannibalizing the father; acting out the Kronos myth. What a rich field for social anthropology this is, or psycho-history.

It is the mystery of Good that needs explaining, not of Evil. The mystery of brotherhood, of man's spiritual longings. It is not unlike the mystery of God—does he exist or is he only a projection of our need, the gauzy scarf we wrap around the skull to disguise our fear of death?

I have been thinking a lot about Henry this week, and how he would have rejoiced at this non-violent revolution if he were alive. Sometimes I think I am compulsively watching the news because he can't, as if I doing it for him.

November 24

I've been too busy to write the past few months, and truth to tell, not very interested in doing so. What is there to say? In my personal sphere, I'm prosperous and content, or maybe just resigned.

The world, of course, is neither. A civil war is raging in Yugoslavia, which Europe is unable or unwilling to stop. Vukovar and Dubrovnik have been heavily shelled; there is much suffering all over the country. The Iraqis are dying of cholera and malnutrition, effects of the war and the sanctions. It is predicted that millions around the world will have died of AIDs by the year 2,000. Hundreds of Haitian corpses are washing up on Florida beaches again. Their economy is more desperate than ever; they too are under sanctions.

I've come to think that sanctions are a dubious idea, possibly an even worse form of warfare than warfare itself. At least war is more or less fought by soldiers, whereas sanctions directly target civilians, with the poorest dying first. It's pure social Darwinism, with the rich playing the role of "the fittest."

Lewis Lapham's definition of politics in the most recent Harper's: "The ceaseless and bitter argument about who has the power to do what to whom, at what price, for how long, and with what chance of redress."

A long letter from Jenine the other day, apologizing for the scantiness of her correspondence. It seems she had a crisis of faith six months ago that led her to debate whether or not to leave the convent. She has come more and more under the influence of the people at Jonah House, I gather, and goes with them to many of their demonstrations. She claims not to be tempted to commit civil disobedience herself, however, seeing herself in a more supportive role. After attending several retreats, she decided to stay on in the order but has requested a transfer to the sister house in Charlottesville, Virginia, where she will continue to teach but also take courses at the university. It sounded like she was turning over a new leaf, though in some ways it looks to me like a compromise: she will remain a nun, but change her surroundings. I hope for her sake that that's all that is needed.

One of the things she explored while on retreat was her strong desire for order and security, which she attributes to losing her mother before she knew her and being raised by an over-protective, depressed grandmother whom she was unable to help. She was deeply affected by Mrs. Abbott's death last year.

I gather she regularly writes to the Ploughshares protestors who are in jail for acts of anti-nuclear civil disobedience. She said she also urges her students to write them, on the grounds that whatever the courts may say, their "crimes" were committed out of principled beliefs. They are like the early Christians, she tells them.

She continues to be bothered by the Church's position on war and the contradiction between that and Jesus' admonition to resist not evil but turn the other cheek. She accepts that the Church had to compromise because of the threat of Islam, and adopt the idea of "Just Wars" which Catholics can fight in, but the concept troubles her. I don't quite see why. If the Christians hadn't defended themselves, they might well have been conquered and absorbed. Who in our century can honestly deny that non-resistance to Hitler would have led to the annihilation of the few good things western civilization has evolved? That's always the stumbling block for me when thinking about pacifism—Hitler.

"*I sometimes wish Henry were here,*" *Jenine said,* "*he had a way of helping me clarify issues; without him I feel I'm left in my natural muddle.*" *I know what she means.*

December 12

Stephen and I are both well again, thank God, after three weeks of a bronchial flu that felt like pneumonia. I swear the world is developing superbugs these days.

The illness has left me tired and depressed, as has the news that Russia is now Yeltsin's "Confederation of Independent States." Somehow I don't trust the man, for all his professions of democracy. Gorbachev is expected to resign any day; in the CBC footage of him tonight he looked so weary and sad it wrung my heart.

Not even Napoleon suffered such a humiliating fall. The Napoleonic Codes, at least, remain, and the Arch de Triomphe, whereas what is left of Gorbachev's dream but ashes? A bankrupt nation, widespread misery, even possible starvation this winter. I took one look at the headlines this morning and my eyes filled with tears. USSR TO DIE ON JANUARY 1, it said. Inside were obituaries for Gorbachev, with pictures of him. I suddenly realized how much he looks like my father, in his younger days before his illness—the same smile, the same twinkle in his eye. It is like losing my father all over again. He is to hand over the keys to the Kremlin and the nuclear arsenal on New Year's Eve. What will become of him? There is no man to whom the world owes a greater debt.

December 19

A few days ago I received the package Jenine sent containing Henry's diaries, but I was too sick to open them. You wait five years and think the wounds have closed, and suddenly out of the blue the government erupts into your life again. So the wounds open and bleed, and ghosts come dancing out.

I have been dreaming about Henry for the past three nights, dreams filled with yearning where we melt into each other and dissolve in a pool of buttery bliss. Orgasmic dreams, which when I wake, leave me feeling bereft. In the one last night we were lying on a bed of deep green moss, near the gates of a cemetery. As if even while making love to him I am aware of the closeness of death.

The diaries and the other papers stirred up old longings, as well as old mysteries. One of the odd things I found in the surveillance file was that typed note in a plain white envelope addressed "To the Abbot Family," which I recognized the minute I saw it. It was the letter I found in the Abbott mailbox at the end of the lane the day after the funeral. I had gone out for a walk to be by myself and saw the red flag sticking up on the mailbox. There was an envelope inside, with no postmark, which meant it had been delivered by hand. When I got back, I gave it to Mrs. Abbott, who read it and then showed it to me.

Now I wonder if she didn't also later show it to Walter, and he turned it over to the investigators. I always thought it strange that the note was unsigned, but I had too many other things to worry about at the time to give it any thought. Now I wonder if its author wasn't the "Mr. X" Henry refers to in his diary. The note reads, "You don't know me, but I wish to extend my deepest sympathies to the members of the Abbott family during this time of tragic loss. I had warm feelings for the man you knew as your son, brother, and uncle. He touched my life, though I was never able to properly thank him. My sincere apologies for intruding on your grief. With warmest wishes,…"

But there was nothing after the comma—no signature, no identification of who had written it. Mother Abbott was as puzzled as I, but I could tell she was moved by what the letter said. Was it "Mr. X" whose life had been touched by his conversations with Henry? It's another thing about the affair of Henry's death that I'll never know.

I had a strange thought just now, connected to a memory of something Stephen said two or three summers ago. Walter must have known Henry's feelings about me: he must have been shown his brother's papers, including the second diary that I didn't know about till yesterday. So he has known for several years, if not before that, that I loved his brother.

The memory that triggered this thought was of a day when Stephen and I took a walk out to the beaver pond. Stephen was tossing stones in the water, watching the circles they made. Without any prelude he asked if I had ever been in love with his Uncle Henry. I concealed my surprise and said no, I hadn't—casually, as if his question was an ordinary one. "I loved him as a friend, as a brother-in-law," I added. Stephen nodded and continued throwing stones. I asked what made him think of Henry and why he should all of a sudden ask if I had been in love with him. He shrugged, I remember, saying it was just something his Dad had said the last time he'd seen him, though what, exactly, he was vague about. I didn't push him, and asked instead if there was something about the beaver pond that made him think of Henry. He said it *was the stream we had followed that leads to the pond, which reminded him of the stream behind the fields at the Abbotts' farm. "Henry used to find stones for me there," he said, and then we didn't say much, both of us lost in memories, mine of that dream I'd had of wading in the stream and finding gold nuggets which I put between my breasts, with Henry on the bank, smiling and saying "I hope you'll save some of those for me." My memories of him are all rather like that, small gold treasures held close and warm between my breasts.*

Philip will be arriving by train from Toronto in a few days, for the Christmas holiday. His flight comes in at noon, which gives him two hours to catch the train. With luck everything should go smoothly. I've purchased the tree, but I'll wait till he's here to set it up. It's something he always likes to do.

I shall concentrate on turkeys and presents and popcorn balls and not let this bolt from the past throw me off balance. Henry could always do that. Mr. Ghost of Christmas Might-Have-Been.

CHAPTER 12

▼

I didn't learn of my Uncle Henry's diaries until the first year of the new century, the summer after I graduated from university. I was spending time with my mother at the lake cottage while waiting for graduate school to start in the fall. There must have been something in the landscape that provoked my dream, but I awoke one morning with a vivid sense of him, which surprised me, for though his death and the manner of it had long bothered me, particularly when I was a child, it hadn't exactly been in the foreground of my consciousness all those years.

In the dream I was wading in a shallow stream that ran beside a cemetery. Suddenly I knew that my uncle Henry was buried there. Then I was standing beside an overgrown mound of earth, looking at a headstone. I pushed aside the weeds to examine it. There was no name, but an inscription, a brief message I couldn't decipher. Half the letters seemed to have been omitted, making the words unintelligible. I kept staring at them, certain it was a code I could crack, but I tried too hard and woke myself up.

After breakfast I asked my mother to tell me what she knew about my uncle's death. She thought for a minute, and then went up to the attic and brought down the diaries and other papers she and Jenine had received through the Freedom of Information Act. I was amazed that only now I was being told of their existence, but then my mother has never much wanted to talk about the past. I had assumed it was freighted for her with memories of her marriage to my father, and the divorce, which she didn't want to relive.

I spent the next several days avidly reading what she gave me, looking, I suppose, for some way of putting my uncle's story together that would make sense, one that would tell me who killed him. The papers did help me form a hypothesis, but unfortunately it's only that, a hypothesis, lacking evidence that would pass muster with a jury. Still, it is a working construct, and that is better than no explanation at all.

The diaries opened my eyes to a different way of seeing my parents' marriage, particularly how hard it must have been for my mother. It seems clear to me that she and Henry might very well have ended up living together if Henry hadn't been killed: in due time, in other words, their foot would have slid. When I asked her this directly, however, she just smiled and shrugged, as if it was an academic question, not worth pursuing.

It didn't come entirely as a surprise to me when I read in my uncle's second diary about his feelings for my mother; I had felt at the time that there was something going on between them. My father had more or less confirmed this one summer when I was down there, the only time I remember him bringing up the subject of Henry. We were sitting out on the back patio having breakfast, and he was looking particularly morose and full of anger, which I thought of back then as being like thick black lava swirling around beneath the surface, ready to erupt. I was frightened of it, but nonetheless, for some reason, instead of ignoring him and getting on with my cereal, I asked him if he was feeling okay and he said no, he wasn't, and proceeded to tell me about this dream he'd had, which was "so stupid it made him angry." In it he and Elizabeth were standing beside his mother's grave, and then suddenly he saw that Henry was standing across from them, and beckoning to Elizabeth for her to come over to where he was. This my father found outrageous; he yelled at Henry that he was dead and had no right to do pull such a stunt over his mother's corpse, whereupon Henry sat down on the tombstone and grinned ("nastily," according to my father) and said, "She's my mother now."

Or words to that effect. I was too dumbfounded to ask what he thought about it; I knew he believed dreams were bullshit. He then surprised me further by saying, "I knew about your mother and Henry all along, you know, did you mother ever tell you that?" No, I said, she hadn't. "Well, I did," he said, and then he went back to reading his newspaper.

Now I wonder if he "knew" because he had read Henry's diaries. He might have been privy to his papers long before we were; he might have seen them as part of the official investigation into his brother's death, been asked to testify to his handwriting, or something. He did, after all, have a Top Secret Security Clearance; for all I know, my uncle's diaries might have been photocopied during the investigation that was ongoing even before his death. I'm sure my father will never tell me, and at this late date, I doubt if it matters.

Since I hope to make films some day (it is, after all, my "academic field"), I keep wondering what kind of film script I would write about my mother's relationship with my uncle. What angle would I take? I suppose that would depend on my prospective audience. If it were done as a made-for-TV film, the romance would be central, with the politics of chemical weapons more or less in the background. If it was an indie film destined for the art houses, which is what I'd like to make, the romance would be a subplot. My film would be a psycho-political thriller, a parable about secrets, lies, and governments, with maybe the theme of chance and fate thrown in for the existentialists in the crowd.

I think I'd start with the scene of the funeral and go backwards to that Fourth of July, 1986. Everyone in the Abbott family would be present at the graveside, plus dozens of other people standing farther at a distance. The presence of these people is unexpected: there had been little publicity about Henry's death in the newspapers.

Who would have thought that my uncle had so many friends in that town? There were people there not only from the town but from the labs, ostensibly to pay their respects to Walter's family, but I think also to show their respect, maybe even affection, for Henry. Or perhaps they were there as a gesture of resistance to government policies, who knows?

Their faces are somber, expressionless. The camera rests for a moment on Grandfather Abbott, who stands beside the grave in a dark shiny suit stretched tight over his belly, holding a black felt hat in his hands. Beside him is my grandmother, looking thin and unwell; within the year she will follow her son to this cemetery, where her daughter Sylvie is also buried. To her left is Jenine, her lovely face veiled, her head bowed.

The camera doesn't linger here; these are minor characters, after all. It's the other four that matter, at least to me, two on each side of the casket that is being lowered into the ground. I stand holding my mother's hand. I am nine years old. My brother Philip stands across from me, with my father. When the funeral is over my mother and I will take the plane to eastern Ontario, where I will spend the rest of my childhood. Her last memory picture of this time, she says, is of Philip's sullen face in the airport terminal, the set of his shoulders as he took our father's hand and turned away.

Our family is splitting up, though I don't know that then. I only know that there is something wrong with my parents' marriage, and that somehow this is connected to the man being buried here. My mother is crying. My father, across from us, seems frozen and indifferent. Philip looks angry and confused. I myself am miserably depressed. I feel abandoned, something I have felt before but never so totally. I know that none of us will be the same again, that it's not just my uncle being buried here.

To this day, no one knows who killed him, whether the Unknown Intruder who shot him was a spy or a terrorist or a thief surprised in the act, or who knows, maybe even an Animal Rights activist who thought there were animal experiments going on there, though it's hard to imagine an Animal Rights person arming himself with a high-powered rifle. One hypothesis is that the assassin was someone hired by the government, or someone who worked at the labs who wanted to get rid of him and lured him in with the ploy of the unlocked gate. Whoever did it was never apprehended, nor was any motive ever offered in explanation.

In addition to the Maryland state police investigation there were several federal ones (FBI, CIA, Defense Intelligence), but though my mother and Jenine tried many times over the years to get information on what happened that night, they never obtained anything from the Freedom of Information office but press clippings they had already clipped themselves. They did receive the papers they confiscated from Henry's apartment, of course, years later, and the field reports of the government investigators, but even these were heavily censored. What the government knew about the shooting, if anything, is still classified.

The press reports from the Washington and Baltimore papers are not lengthy. One is captioned *"Longtime Protestor Shot Outside Gate of Edgewood Laboratories,"* but this isn't strictly accurate. From what my mother told me, Henry's body was found *inside* the gate, not outside. As she reconstructs it, Henry must have gone at 4:30 that morning to meditate for a while before greeting the incoming work shift, which was apparently his usual pattern every morning. When he arrived he found the guard-post mysteriously empty of guards, and the gate mysteriously unlocked. Curious or concerned, or both, he must have ventured inside, where he saw something. Either that, or someone who was about to enter one of the buildings saw him. Whoever it was fired at him from thirty yards and then fled through the open gate.

This, although plausible, raises further questions. The gates had never been left unmanned before, let alone unlocked: where the guards were at the time the shots were fired has never been explained. The post was definitely unmanned though, my mother insists on this, and she insists that Henry's body was found inside not outside the gates, a point borne out by the early police reports. An intruder up to no good, such as a spy or a terrorist, may have killed my uncle, but if the gates were unmanned, it had to have been at least partly an inside job. There had to have been collusion: the guards and the Intruder must have worked together—unless the Intruder forced the guards to unlock the gate, then killed them, and the government conveniently disposed of their bodies, which seems a bit much to swallow: more likely, the guards were bribed to unlock the gates, or ordered to by a superior. But bribed or ordered by whom? Presumably by the same people that were paying the gunman, or spy, or thief, or terrorist, or whatever. The mystery of the absent guards is not addressed in any of the press reports, an omission which seems suspicious.

Another hypothesis that could be played with in a screenplay is the character of Gentleman X, the researcher at the labs referred to in my uncle's diaries. What if he was a double agent of some kind, and cracking under the strain? What if he was doing one last job for whatever government he was working for (Iran, Israel?) and unexpectedly saw Henry.... No, that would lead too far afield, into John le Carre territory.

It was in the U.S. government's interest, of course, to have the episode hushed up: they wouldn't want any publicity about so flagrant and dangerous a security breach. No doubt they also wanted to protect the public from any "undue alarm" they might feel if it were known that an armed intruder had penetrated the gates of a chemical weapons research lab.

Another of my theories, about why my Aunt Jenine was questioned about my uncle's whereabouts on the 4th of July, is supported by the surveillance notes the field agents kept on my uncle in the weeks before his death. I pored over these for hours, as if they were the clue to the code in my dream. Most of each page was blacked out, but piecing together what was left led me to the conclusion that the Internal Security men were at that time investigating Henry as part of a larger investigation into my father, who I believe was suspected of a security leak. They seemed to think he was using my mother as a conduit to transmit information to Henry, who in turn was presumably transmitting it to Jonah House and from thence to their imaginary "Communist world," which they unjustly suspected the Berrigans of having ties with. In other words, they suspected my whole family, all of whom were kept under surveillance. My parents' phones were tapped, which my mother says she suspected at the time. What she didn't know was that her car was followed that day when she went to Henry's to return his diaries, or that she was followed home when she left. The security detail parked beside her when she went in to the 7 & 11 for cigarettes. "Subject returns to car with a carton of Virginia Slims," the note says. My mother never noticed them.

I would have this as a scene in my film, though on second thought it might look too much like that one in *The China Syndrome,* where a mysterious car waits for Jack Lemmon outside the post office. Mine wouldn't involve any car chases, though, just an image of the unguarded innocence of people who are unknowingly subjects of surveillance.

The case of my uncle Henry was closed long ago. In a sense how he died doesn't matter, certainly not to the public. No materials or files were stolen from the Edgewood labs that night, no terrorist set off any nerve-gas or any of the other lethal chemicals they were working on in there. Still, I think if my film reconstructed my Uncle Henry's death, I would play it as heroic. I'd have him somehow wrestle with the Unknown Intruder, and injure him in some way that prevents him from carrying out his plan.

Here's the scene sequence: Henry wrestles the man to the ground. He loses the struggle and is eventually strangled, but he has succeeded in disarming the attacker, who flees and the terrorist action is foiled. The camera focuses on the Intruder's face, in close-up, as he rests, panting, beside a tree. It has been blackened with charcoal, his head obscured by a knit cap, but we know him, don't we? He is one of the government agents who questioned my Aunt Jenine. No, he is Double Agent X that Henry lunched with in that restaurant on the Eastern Shore. No again: he is my father, who has manufactured an opportunity to finally rid himself of his troublesome little brother, whose whole existence is a standing rebuke to the way he lives...

But I am waxing melodramatic, slipping into comic book mode. In fact, the man who killed my uncle is not anyone the audience knows. He is not black, not Middle Eastern, just a man, with a mean, fanatical face. He kills my uncle with a high-powered rifle from fifty yards. There is no bodily contact, nothing resembling a heroic struggle.

It wouldn't be in character anyway for Uncle Henry to have wrestled a killer to the ground, he would more likely have tried to engage him in dialogue, but however it actually happened, I will always see my uncle as a hero. I loved him and admired him. He was an honest, honorable man.

I spent the rest of my growing up in the small Ontario town where my grandmother lived until she died in 1989. The landscape around isn't too different from the farmland in Maryland, except in the winter, when it stays white much, much longer. Politics up here, of course, is very different. For one thing there's not the same sense of urgency: it's not your government that's running, and ruining, the planet, so it tends to be more laid back.

My mother is running her own real estate office now. As far as I know her life up here has been a happy one, even though she never remarried. She has lately taken up the piano; she also does environmental work, and is on the board of the town museum. I gather she is even considering running for a seat on the town council next year.

My brother Philip is at law school, presumably doing well; we don't communicate much. Aunt Jenine is back teaching in Baltimore. I go down to see her now and again, when I check in on my grandfather, who is in a nursing home there. He's not very responsive these days, but his eyes light up sometimes when I show him my stones. I still collect them.

My father I don't see much of. In fact, I haven't been down to Edgewood for years. My grandfather sold Abbottsford when he went into the home, about the same time Philip went off to university and my father sold our old house. He lives in one of these classy high-rises now, on one of the top floors where if he ever sees Maryland's "faraway meadows rich with corn, clear on the cool September morn," it's through window glass. Though I imagine meadows don't do much for him one way or the other; he prefers air-conditioned air, pumped through metal pipes.

I don't see much point in trying to communicate with my father. Maybe I'll give it a shot when I'm thirty, but right now it doesn't seem worth the hassle. He's not likely to have changed since the last time I saw him. He still works at the lab, designing weapons.

Since Henry's death nothing much has changed on that front; the chemical weapons factories have not gone out of business, despite the treaties. What we know now that we didn't then is exactly how abominable Russian attack plans were in the eighties. Not only did their MIRV'd missiles carry hydrogen bombs, they also carried delayed-action chemical and bacteriological weapons designed to spread plagues that would kill off whatever wretched survivors were left from the initial nuclear strikes.

I often wonder if Henry would have kept on with his vigils if he had known all that. I suspect so, perhaps in the hope that on the other side some counterpart Russian soul was doing the same thing. Faithful to the end in believing that the individual could leaven the loaf, that as Thoreau's wrote, "It is not important that the right should always triumph, but that there *be* right, to keep things at least somewhat in balance." Thoreau, the original ecologist, knew how essential balance was.

978-0-595-40016-4
0-595-40016-7

Lightning Source UK Ltd.
Milton Keynes UK
UKHW010637030520
362638UK00001B/35

9 780595 400164